THE SELF-DEVOTED FRIEND

THE SELF-DEVOTED FRIEND

MARVIN COHEN

TOUGH POETS PRESS
ARLINGTON, MASSACHUSETTS

ISBN 978-0-692-87281-9
Tough Poets Press
49 Churchill Avenue, Floor 2
Arlington, Massachusetts 02476
U.S.A.

www.toughpoets.com

To Candace Watt

A SEEMINGLY SCIENTIFIC EXPLANATION
OF *THE SELF-DEVOTED FRIEND*

Every person, at the moment he feels or wants or decides something, is simultaneously being contradicted or challenged by his accompanying "other self." This sounds like self-warfare, but it's also harmony or cooperation, hence the title *The Self-Devoted Friend*. In Great Britain's Parliament, this is like "Her Majesty's backbench loyal opposition" (to the currently ruling members sitting in front). So I divide the self of every person in two, and the endless conversation throughout life ensues. I get an impulse for action, and it's answered by my inner "friend," with hardly any hesitation. Physically, we're "forked" creatures with our torsos split into two legs divided at the top. So too, we're emotionally split with a thesis and an antithesis in two prevailing choruses, endlessly singing counterpoint.

The hum inside our heads. Bickering or augmenting, it's our systematic togetherness, like homeostasis and the warfare of trying to see things through and set them straight, problem solving, working things out (or not). Trying to settle issues, aiming for the comfort zone, two idea-trains vying for solutions on two intertwining tracks. Blending may be temporary bliss, but the combatting is a work in progress. Definitions of living proceed from our self-devoted friend's nuclear duality. Hardly quite on the same page, but those pages multiply as the lungs counter-breathe; and footsteps alternate right to left, neither slacking in their joint enterprise. Voice set both to and against voice, the duality pulsing out through fun's respite and livelihood's desperation.

Marvin Cohen
New York City, 2017

IN THE BEGINNING, THERE WAS NOTHING. That led to my friend. The world was formed, the earth shaped, space made finite, stars stuck in their place, and the cell of life germinated in the sea. After the first creation, the embodiment of life grew into a complex culmination, many cells gathered together, and birth blessed itself with that original stroke of piety, the human being. God was crowned King, history corrupted the pages of mankind, and rivals on the stage of greatness claimed immense dowries into marriage with death, while power survived to bleed their remaining subjects. A crucial energy arrived. Behold: my friend.

* * *

My friend's mother and my friend's father, before they knew each other, were strangers like other people. That much can be said for them. Unknown to my friend, they met one day. Romance bloomed, and they made a fatal date. When the man showed up, he wasn't alone. My friend was already in him, but the man nervously concealed it.

My friend began to poke about, or stir, and when his bearer kissed the woman, the moment of transference was at hand. My friend was bodily relocated, and by the time the romantic ceremonies were concluded, and the sentimental note of goodbye had been struck, the man was devoid of my friend, and the woman was briefly full of him.

His environment changed, my friend developed strangely in the new person by whom—a little self-consciously—he was being carried about. He came into his own, as his birth had to be arranged. He was a man about it, found deliverance, and was out cold. Although his own man now, he was much babied; and began possessing independent character traits, like naiveté.

* * *

Introduced to the world by birth, my friend had a great deal of ignorance to defend. Now he has less, but experience has yet to violate an almost pre-existing state of innocence. Daily my friend collects facts to punctuate his emotions, while compiling an album of memory. His biology is already over-ripely mature, and life is dragging him beyond the slow knowledge-encumbered mind that remains blindly faithful to his wise ignorance. His learning only serves to document his backslide to the conservative innocence that keeps control over his origin. Time runs him out of motion, and he's beguiled by neveranywhere: a point where time resides.

* * *

Having begun to live, my friend was safely born. After a normal start, his life underwent development. At that point, everything turned out wrong. He was able to be puzzled. Now, it's all hopeless. The pain itself laughs, while he looks on with vague amusement. "This is total," he at least says. The next problem is whether to agree. He consults his hunches, and slowly becomes undecided. This is his firm decision. Having chosen it, he decisively prolongs its defense.

* * *

Looking back, he says, "My birth was hardly timely, considering what year it was. After that, conditions grew worse, God only knows. As for being born, there was little my mother could do about it, and I stretched this malicious opportunity to the utmost. What else could I do? A man's got to live, whether he's born or not. If he's born, so much the worse, as far as worldly happiness goes. If not, then life is simplified, and grows heavenly every day. This is my philosophy, though it be my death and defile that angry hour when my birth helplessly shrieked, making a last-ditch effort to consume itself in a mortal pact of suicide prior to the unfolding of the world's primrose idealism, where the trouble and fire-works start, penetrating each waking nerve and budding impulse until we're stung to prolong our elaborate mistake in heroic martyrdom to a cause initially betrayed. So I became life's slave, and sold my birth into all conditions, penile servitude and the dire luxury of enforced poverty that burns up my wealth and mints the ashes into further torture. So what? I had my fun too." Then, you should see him smile!

* * *

My friend made a great effort at being born, and didn't succeed until the last minute. By then, it was almost too late. His mother had given herself up to the resignation of fate, and found herself somewhere else at the time. It was heroic of my friend, under such a handicap, to come up as far as he did, and survive with his single-minded intensity, almost single-handedly. Surely life should have rewarded him for this immense effort, his courageous will. But what ensued was mere punishment, and a continual hell. Here at last was pure irony, and a tragedy of splendid proportions. Undaunted, however, my friend lived a comedy, and for every tear splashed laughter. The moral? There is no moral, since my friend resists morality of any kind or description. For his own benefit, where his kindness both begins and ends. Is that selfish of him? Think of all the time he wasted if it isn't. Having made the bargain at birth, he continued to buy life out to the last, and paid with the current money and hard cash of himself. It was a fair deal, cheating both sides, and being broke against the middle. Much later on, the deal was void, but then it was too late, like the marching hour of his death-birth. Meanwhile, preoccupied in being alive, he lives himself right out of existence with such fanaticism he's back again to practice the perfection and convince the actual of itself. It takes some doing.

* * *

Is my friend actual? At any rate, he certainly lives. Can anything less be said about a man?

My friend devotes himself to his life, whenever he can find the spare time. His motto is: "Don't just sit there: Live!" So he's too busy to stand, to walk, to do anything, except to live. He even refused to kiss a girl, when invited, on the grounds that it was time again to be living. Schedules are sacred to him.

And what else? Certainly more. There's more to living than just life, and my friend is possessed by just that extra something, or, to put it another way, that something extra, little or large, by which my friend exceeds his own scale. And how!, I may add.

My friend is supercolossal, on a grand scale. An important addition to humanity, it's an understatement to say that he merely lives. He exists as well, and is equally versatile in indulging both states of being, which makes him ultradimensional, to say the barren least, the most minimum least. In fact, he's a phenomenon, it can safely be realistically said. Truth itself would verify this, and heap extra substantial actuality on my already much-proven friend, who would shrink in modesty from these flattering bouquets of redundancy. Suffice it, that he is.

But isn't there more to it than that? Surely truth must be lurking somewhere, heaping glamorous fact all over "is." Or is that an exaggeration?

The truth is a glorious fact, although frequently too good to be true. A great deal of truth is attached to my friend, revealing his character as well as describing him accurately, in a wealth of realistic exaggeration, exposing the merciless details about his life, especially what is current, momentary, and in the present. This is positively no lie, as one look at my friend in the straight glaring light of honesty can palpably prove, simply slaughtering doubt. There he actually is, a moving, literal representation of his living self, itself, brimful of very essence, unself-limiting in totality of scope and depth, and weirdly confounding imagination. This truth is so packed with substance, fact is crowded out, being superfluous to that considerable thing, my friend.

As an appearance? Being appears itself.

Directly inside his life lives the living version of my friend, approximating himself as his own most reasonable facsimile. This true-to-life duplicate is so original, that it outdoes reality with an almost superhuman realism, so naturalistic that nature is put to shame. Just how genuine is my friend? The image is so precise, down to the finest, most delicately chiseled detail, shaded in trembling halftone and delineated by perfect art in the discipline of strict science, that you can almost hear the breathing, and can practically sense a whole heart absorbed in thump and beat. The hair seems to shine in light, and gives the incredible illusion of growing. The lips look wet! Motion is about to move, and the feeling can actually be felt! Who'll deny that here's my friend represented by life? Who isn't convinced that life itself realizes its ultimate proxy in the person of my friend? This is no secondhand reproduction, this is vitality self-created. The very thoughts are visible, magnifying truth in transparent brain cells. The soul is illuminated, God's sun, upon the highest authority. Here is being, purified by essence, himself, my friend.

* * *

Before my friend was even a stranger to me, I hardly knew him. Not that I snobbed him. It wasn't necessary. We hadn't been properly introduced, the pleasure of our acquaintance hadn't been arranged, and we were far from speaking terms. We gave each other the silent treatment, which was our most harmonious relationship by far, although ignorance absentmindedly prevented us from enjoying it. We were well off, but cursed with premature innocence. This was the fatal condition that set off that inevitable accident, our meeting. Ever since then, we've been trying to recover together, but have only accelerated the impact of our being jointly the double mutual victims of that singular merger.

To take some of the heat off, I trapped him into conversation, and got him talking about life (right down my alley, since I was living it myself). He spoke of life, though, as something to distinguish us apart. This wasn't fair to one of us, so we began a lifelong competition, to see who would survive, and who was fit to be eliminated. So all subsequent hostility, in this framework, can't be surprising, and can be justified under the description of natural, considering that there was one life between us, and two totally full persons desperately craving to live it. What could be sweeter, under those circumstances, than our greedy antagonism, vicious rivalry, and occasional guilty lapses into friendship, selfishly intertwined with sympathetic mutuality, by which we were doubled or halved? Meanwhile life stood by, watching the contest, and decidedly undecided. Were we fighting for nothing?

"Were it not for life," my friend gravely admitted, "I shouldn't be here today to tell about it." "About what?" said I. "Oh mind your own business," he said, peeved. "It's your life, not mine," I observed, shrugging faintly my shoulder. As a result, closing began to be done by his eyes to themselves, which shut out the remaining light and switched on artificial darkness. "You can't face life," I said, serving truth on a dish of malice. "That's the nice part about it," he said, smug. Conceited for all his vanity, he cultivated his ignorance like a garden where nothing grows, and exposed it to all weathers. To make sure, he carries a little umbrella about with him, in case he should happen to rain. But I expect him to pour, despite the sunny expression he always keeps arranging through his sneaky smile, fair-weather friend that he is.

* * *

"You fascinate me," I told my friend: "Couldn't you tell me something about yourself: your habits, appearance, dress, political opinions, hobbies, or, any other eccentricities you care to mention in passing? I'd make a grateful audience. And a deeply appreciative one, too."

My friend, flattering me, and slandering himself, began (making truth potent, for there was so much to be true about, and so many lies standing by unemploymently available as hit-and-miss substitutes, if truth should grow a heart attack and die by the wayside singing its own funeral praises and mourning itself with false tears of insincerity and a heart dissembling grief, shouting, "To thine own self be true, you rotten faker!"):

"When the sky is wondrous, and the weather excels, I have to read about it. I never look up more than twice a day, except for an emergency.

"My appearance takes on a familiar aspect the more it is looked at.

"My face is cute, except that the features belong on another person. My clothing, immaculately imperfect, fits half my length; on the other half is the thrift of nudity—scandalous designs in skin and hair.

"Politically I am ambidextrous, and usually switch to the man elected.

"For hobby, I hitchhike around the block. Then, for exercise, I walk home."

"Thank you," I said: "Now I know all about you." "Not all." "You mean you've left something out? What? I've got to know." "I'll tell you another time," promised my friend, and dove disappearingly into the waiting vehicle of the future. It rode him away. I puzzle the remains.

* * *

Wearing his life in top shape, my friend used his mind frequently in the act, introducing one thought to another by an almost daily process; and wherever gaps developed, filling the while from a supply of the most endless emotions that kept pulse pace with his breathing duration. Living gave an uncommon sensation, full of strange and startling effects that only the starkly familiar is able to pull off; and bobbing on the surface would be the shield of identity, behind which my friend would courageously hide, being internal all the time. One's self! What subjective possibilities this unleashed! And while this implausible world underwent its unrecorded history, surviving event after shocking event, don't forget imagination, improvising itself continuously and giving shape to the ups and downs and sidewhirls from what we must vaguely call motion, leading to conservative change. How intimate to live one's life. It certainly clashes with external things—a mirror, for instance. Inside himself on all levels, the central factor of his variety, my friend did and thought what his life excused him to do and think, and so lived in the large freedom of his prison. "How's life?" I asked him, getting personal all of a sudden. His smile filled with so many ambiguities, it never graduated from his frown, and the face was glowing with a neutral emotion. "Never mind," I advised, a suggestion which he eagerly took to heart, carrying out at once.

By never minding, my friend kept increasing his vacuum, almost annihilating himself. To save his life, I had to remind him to be what he already was, namely selfish.

My friend's memory is so bad, he continually forgets to exist. This is dangerous, and could lead to death. "Think of yourself," I warned him, "and act on it." By following this advice, he became selfish. Sacrificed completely to self, my friend has forgotten all about his own life, which, left unguarded, is busy pursuing the ultimate vanity of freedom.

As concerns his self, there's such a thing as overdoing the self business, and, selfishly, my friend is overdoing the overdoing, while his self is frantically trying to catch up. Meanwhile, my friend is left to pursue the waste of an entire lifetime lacking the basic minimum self, which he's too busy being to allow it to be.

Almost my definition, my friend refuses to be anything but what he is. All day long, he's continually being himself. Finally, day gets tired, rests: night comes. And yet, there's my friend, still being himself. "Don't you ever stop?" I asked. "It's too late now," he said, and kept right on, absorbed in his specialty, spending his whole single-minded devotion on the task ahead. One expects that he'll even die as himself, should he ever get that far. At the rate he's going, why not? More consistent miracles have happened.

And now at last it's an allergy, that has reached the incurable stage, and even threatens to survive, providing my friend doesn't chicken out and let the allergy function without a body to stand on; due to, imagine, death afflicting my allergy-smitten friend and ruining all but the allergy itself: into which my friend is incorporated as a temporarily junior partner with a gradually decreasing rank as the business succeeds, he eventually winding up as the waste basket for the office boy he was before the demotion fell due as an added bonus for his superfluously negative contributions to a rundown firm without a profit to its bankrupt name, and in which he's held so many illicit shares that he violates every law in the country and is fired for sheer selfishness, an outcome poetically in justice and meritoriously deserved, and finally he's forced to retire. But not without protest, however. He'd really quit before that.

My friend has a steady season-in, season-out allergy: himself. He really doesn't dare draw quite near, but is afflicted by transmission and other forms of contact. The symptoms range from short-range sneezing to a long-term evolution of vanity. When exposed to himself looking into the mirror, the skin of my friend's image is subject to an hysterical outgrowth of pimples. And as disease is contagious by reflection, my friend's true flesh captures the example of the mirror.

Anti-self serum and ego-killer pills have afforded only external relief. And the personality lessons have merely deformed his character.

He needs to get away from himself. But business affairs, despite his poverty, require his undivided attention. His presence creates a general notion of good will, and is considered one of his personal assets. Meanwhile, his health shoots lower from worse to magni-worse. This may set off an automatic vacation, a solution so tragically overdue that either a humble ghost will result, or an angel addicted to sneezing.

This can't be rushed. My friend isn't even afforded the liberty of suicide without applying for permission from himself. And the red tape is binding. Spies are so alert, he can do nothing behind his back. The miraculous flower of this confusion is honesty.

Honestly, the allergy is a living handicap. It explodes, and my friend is formed. Bang! Essence sweeps him into his incredible version of being, a momentous freak, dwarfed by his own gigantism. His total character is a compensation, in direct loss of his self-gain. Even identity couldn't identify him any better.

Did my friend ever have a handicap? Yes, himself. But in spite of it, in spite of it, he's learned to compensate, to make the absolute most of what remains. So with terrific courage, he's learned to do all his living in defiance of his crippling handicap. No wonder he's unique. In fact, it would be monstrous if he weren't. He goes about, and people stare and wonder. "How does he do it?" their curiosity may be summed. He's a freak. But the oddest thing is, he has no idea. He's normal, thinks he. This is possibly the most staggeringly incredible misassumption ever conceived by any erroneous man's brain in the long or short history of the human world, bar none, and will confound abnormal psychologists from now until the day after the last day of the final end of the finish of everyone's termination. And yet, my friend dares to smile! His teeth have no brains in them, but there they are, exposed to the public, like a bunch of burlesque queens so stripped that nudity and nakedness are prudish, super-religious, and modest by comparison. And *still* he smiles! However, he's handicapped. This is the only reason why he hasn't been arrested, hung, shot, killed, lynched, made to die, poisoned, crucified, quartered, shit upon, choked, beaten, bitten, and subjected to the most hideous extremities of which torture is diabolically capable. His handicap protects him. People take one look at his handicap and form a universal retreat, shouting wild and inane things. They run, without bothering to find a direction. They become beasts, and devour their offspring. They go to psychiatrists. Their psychiatrists go to them. The world itself, having been invented and discovered a billion times, besides having posed for its portrait and been told to smile for the benefit of so many amateur flashbulb photographers on Sundays alone, stops. It stops turning. Everything stops, arms, gestures, legs, everything. Or at least slows down, so my friend finishes smiling. Then normality resumes itself. Cars go off, pedestrians are caught in traffic, policemen make routine arrests. Women sell their legs and bosoms in marriage compacts. The seasons spring down on us, and fall away, at intervals. Money fornicates money, creating monstrous offspring. The man on the street keeps getting modern, in pace with the calendar, and fashion chases women to the length of their sunny lives, blessing the diversities of mediocrity and simple mentalities everywhere. Religion sends off prayer after prayer, unanswered. My friend's smile is a thing of the past. He's all involved in being what he is: a walking handicap. There he goes, consisting of the handicap that's more real than anything else about him, like the soul in the form of a jockey riding an aging horse. The horse gives birth to a series of replacements in the same race, but the jockey gets younger as the race tumbles along, surviving generations of horses that roar down the centuries while the jockey is as fresh as ever, urging toward the finish that never comes, despite layers of geological turf being kicked up by all the legs under him, successive and unending. So goes that distinctive handicap, my friend.

* * *

My friend belonged to a club. He was its member. It was so exclusive, it was private. Once a week, he would hand himself an envelope that contained his weekly membership dues. Later, the club broke up, due to internal friction. He submitted his resignation, and now his loneliness is waged on an informal basis of anarchy. Ruined, possibly forever, is that gay, secure *sense of belonging*. Perhaps a political party, or a marriage pact—or, if necessary, Alcoholics Anonymous? No, why be lost? Instead he turned to me. "Befriend me, will you?" So we paired our lonelinesses, and are doubly destroyed.

* * *

My friend kept having a lonely feeling. So I introduced him to thousands of people, millions and billions of people, even people who were dead or weren't yet born, because I didn't want to discriminate. And now my friend was enjoying all sorts of social lives, at parties, gatherings, dates, conferences, stray meetings, ceremonies, dedications, get-togethers, clubs, observances, parades, wakes, weddings, births, processions, houses of worship, houses of ill and good fame, accidental encounters, chance reacquaintances, anniversaries, appointments, interviews, celebrations, and other loosely defined gregarious occasions that kept him well occupied with people. I could barely see him, because people were always in the way. His loneliness seemed outnumbered. It went into hiding, and rendered only token guerrilla resistance from its isolated underground movement. But it's organized, and is waiting for a ripe moment to declare revolution. Meanwhile, everybody knows my friend. They visit him. He visits them. Long, short, fat, thin, men, ladies. Old, young. As long as they're people, my friend will tolerate anyone, especially everyone. His popularity is so big, that the human race seems minute by comparison. The bellies of pregnant mothers and the tombs of cemeteries help to take up the slack, to keep my friend occupied until reinforcements come. If this is insufficient my friend will have to compromise himself by making friends with the lower animal orders, and, in a pinch, cultivate the whole vegetable kingdom. Old dead Darwin is advising him on the matter. If necessary, evolution will have to undergo expansion. The earth will move over, and make room.

By comparison with others, my friend became snobby. He had to, unless his sense of inferiority would smudge his pride with truth, and deprive him of his *superior status*—his favorite myth, and immensely costly to maintain. He devoted a lifetime, in fact, to elevate its falsehood from the ground level of its obvious absurdity. Although his superior status makes him only slightly average, he protects it with kid gloves, and wouldn't let anyone close enough to be contaminated by it. That takes guts, nerve, and filthy vanity. The ego soared above him, and hardly condescended to even approach such a commonplace liar as a mirror, which it would arrogantly refer to as "that vulgar glass."

My friend is slightly to the center of average, which appeals to his over-refined sense of snobbery. Scanning the mirror one morning, he decided to go into one of his superior fits: He snubbed his own image! Hurt, in fact wounded, the image sank deeper into its glass shell. Altogether, it stopped reflecting him. This pleased my friend, for it left him unique and unrepeated.

His mind was basking in self-consciousness. He wouldn't let one thought slip by without examining its style, rank, efficiency, and degree of loyal dedication to himself. What followed was a general purge, followed by a vote of confidence. Always the same constitutional monarchy was upheld, the royal ego and legislative reason. Assured of domestic stability, my friend only needed a war.

So he found me, and declared it. I declared it right back at him. Then a peace conference created enough differences to be ironed out. Meantime, we were busily balancing power, until all diplomacy was exhausted. Erecting a two-sided mirror right on our borders, we punched a hole in the center, and made ugly faces through it. A mutual concern for aesthetics necessitated armistice. What rejoicing there was!

* * *

"Let's talk politics," I implored my friend. "Good, I'll be delighted to." Then we argued. So we borrowed two television sets, and we switched them both on to the same channel. They faced each other, and my friend and I sat back to back looking at one each. A newscaster came on, presenting the same image for us both. He said something national. Then international. Then even local. Finally he wiped his glasses, and shaved himself for a commercial. The commercial was his most profound comment on human affairs. Because he bled at the chin, a symbol that the world somewhere was bleeding. That ended the program. A very somber note. My friend shut off his set, and I mine. This unanimous act was simultaneous for us both. Then, in reasonable tones, we discussed all the implications that had just been communicated to us. My friend vowed, on God's mercy, that he would never shave himself again. While proclaiming this, he stroked his chin in a most significant fashion. I watched him avidly, aware of his every move. All the while, we were sitting down. Two chairs faced each other. One contained him, the other me. The importance of this is overwhelmingly easy to be overlooked. It directly symbolized man's isolation. He, isolated from me. I, on the contrary, was equally isolated from him. It was, so to speak, a double isolation of which he and I were joint halves. This geometry points to one conclusion: Democracy, whereby identical men are in some respects similar, treats all differences alike, which means that anyone can participate. Provided you were born human, and not only stay that way, but promise to screw your partner with humanity-seed, to assure yourself and others of human rat-race survival. My friend and I discussed all this calmly. The world stirred, and then grew still. Frankly, we felt so totally alive, that we scarcely differed in our breath. Our eyes recorded the scene with almost photographic precision. Out one window, the sun was threatening to set. Believing in common beauty for all, we let it.

* * *

My friend was standing still, absorbed in vaguely doing nothing. Not even the environment was well defined; the weather was unclear; in fact, his heredity was dubious.

"Doing anything?" I asked him. "Can't you see I'm busy?" he lied, and pretended to be thinking about something. However, his hands were so idle, that they were getting unemployment insurance. And his feet were so shiftless, they just stood there, too lazy even to tap rhythm to an inner tune or melody. In fact, they didn't even support the legs or body, despite being legally married to them. So it is not surprising to consider that my friend had a "floating" feeling.

"You should do something about your lethargy," I reminded him. Quick to take a hint, he fell asleep. He woke up remarkably improved.

Indebted to sleep for his improvement, he paid his debt by going to sleep again. Whatever was easiest, he followed, which led him directly to inertia, a state of inactivity in which he instantly rejoiced, and devoted all his energy to, eagerly, without fear of waste or stint of duty. At last he had a cause, a goal, a direction to absorb his vast flow, discipline his talents, and concentrate his capacities. Life took on meaning, and he came alive, and gave his living vividness into the hands of sleep, where inertia felt most at home. How noble, now that he had something to do. His idle days were over. His enthusiasm obsessed him.

A standard blob of mass-produced dreams became his easy-as-breathing product. No wastrel was this on-the-ball hustler. He was quick to seize his mission, obey the sacred summons of his calling. It was the only true vocation. Soon his dreams were the symbol of one man's perseverance in industry, and an example to our frivolous youth. Only by dark oblivious channels was he even approximately emulated.

* * *

"I'm in love with the law of inertia," said my friend, and to prove his point, taking the trouble to be his own illustrator, slipping practice into theory like a buzz saw into a loaf of prisoner's bread, he converted his activity to sleep practically without transition, which had a slow and settling effect to which he succumbed, keeping pace with his sleep. "Notice that I'm not awake," he said, commenting like a tourist guide whose elaborate description is concerned with the interior of the bus and rendered more dramatic by the absence of windows, reducing the outside world to rumor, memory, and unreality while that object of curiosity, the bus, is parked in slow motion in on itself, so that its driver and four tires are merely ornamental effects, illusion-supporting props to dupe the tourist into momentary truth. "Are you really asleep?" I found myself asking, and never did existence seem more improbable, or probably impossible, as when I watched my friend watching himself sleep, like two spies being spied upon by somebody who is neither a spy nor a person, but just an object so continually looked-at that it grows its own eyes merely to follow the action and keep up to date with the news that happens to take place in the wake of attention.

Since he really was asleep, he didn't answer me, which was far more proof than I ever even wanted to need, let alone had to accept. So I whispered on tiptoes, not omitting to take the tongue of my shoes off, in order to create a silence that would be inaudible, as well as hard to hear. I succeeded. But he woke up, disturbed by my unnatural concern, like a butterfly responding to excessive peace in a war-torn world, whose bombs are at a lull, due to everybody being dead at once, even the live ones, as well as those who are still being neutral on behalf of the safety that would have protected them if the war had had the decency to go local instead of spreading its greed quite universally everywhere. "I'm awake now," my friend estimated, with dream-like faith that life still had enough differences for a man to analyze himself apart with the confidence that he'd be put together again as soon as he just stopped thinking or being used by thought on a twenty-four hour basis for every idle working day while under the influence of nature and subject to its freak laws by which he is forever dominated and is given no vote in the matter, no voice or choice, but is terrorized by things like gravity, conservation, inertia, and other restrictions on the freedom that his soul claims for its original destiny.

"Will you continue to be awake?" I asked. "Yes, because it's so easy," said my friend, who prefers minimum resistance to the hazards of self-penalizing willpower. "God, I've got a lot of energy now," he went on, and I nervously smiled to keep him from thinking that I was scared. Violence, and its twin brother Destruction, are very playful when not asleep, and promote danger after rest has restored them to the peaceful evil that yields an outcrop of heightened diabolical activity. I ran away so fast, that my speed was left behind, which my friend looked at as a trace by which he might powerfully remember me, even if death itself should be the scene of our eventual re-meeting, an outcome it pained me to know it was out of my capacity to avoid. "Wait, I'll be there," came his remaining voice, which, despite my ability to hide, has come following me everywhere.

* * *

My friend has a great deal of unused talent. He is careful to keep it unused. This increases his "potential" quota. He justifies his inactivity under the motto, "Better latent than never."

Everywhere he goes, he saves energy. He does this by being painstakingly idle. That's how all his energy is stored up.

A nuclear fissionist wanted to split him. So he studied ballet lessons, and did an effortless split. He has yet to come up.

In the meantime, his energy is so vast, that it is near to overflowing. What a power-packed potential dynamo he is!

For example, he had a girlfriend, and they went to bed. By the time he was through with her, her ashes were flown away to India.

He once read a book, and applied his energy. Hitler gave him a medal for book burning. That began his anti-intellectual crusade.

He even eats with energy, converting the food back to their original animals. Then when he goes to the bathroom, the city is alerted for a gas mask raid.

When he needs be, he's industrious all right. If for example he walks, the left and right legs in rotation stir up a windmill, and grind his own flour. This is the staff he's bred on. All his life.

And again, when he sleeps, it's with a terrific impact. The bed is never the same ever after, and has to be replaced.

But the more he uses (energy) the more he keeps. This is a miser's instinct. He almost got arrested for usury.

Currently, he's planning to form an energy bank. People can apply to him. He fills them up, and gets half the world pregnant. The birth rate is so speeded, that Darwin can become obsolete overnight.

Sometimes he rests. But not idly.

* * *

My friend had a cold, which encouraged him to practice sneezing. He sneeze-sprayed so many germs, that the flowers were pollinated that way, and ditched all bees. This revolutionized nature, especially the field of botany.

In fact, he sneezed out so many germs, he created a new race: germans. They organized, became a country, and warred on anyone. This was a hideous deal of bad luck for France, but my friend didn't know at the time.

One day, my friend sneezed a little too boldly. A brittle old lady was directly in the path, and died next day of cancer.

This tragedy so overwhelmed my friend, that now he sneezes internally. The germs go in one nostril, out the other, and thereafter they're on their own.

Once on a farm my friend sneezed. It was seeding time, and you should have seen the crops that year. Even the scarecrows got scared.

But now my friend is refined in the way he sneezes. He shoves the cold back down his throat, where it gets intertwined in the intestines, until the ass goes into a ferocious sneeze, creating havoc and wrecking the toilet bowl. However, authorities consider this method backward.

Nor does this daunt my friend. He's a natural innovator. He's busy inventing a spare nose, in case sneezing ruins the first.

Then, he has a collection of every germ-species he's ever sneezed. He distills the essence of each, and makes perfume and wine from them. Thus he's a profiteer.

Of course, he must increase his capital. So, in a part-time hospital laboratory, he's exploring methods of perpetuating the common cold. It may be good for humanity, but business is ruining that abstract phenomenon of his body, health. The thing he dies with, no less. Or lives to painfully protect, in the soul's instrumental utility. And up high, that eager nose. Quivering, on impulsive behavior, whether to eschew or promote the breeze of a new sneeze. Ring out the nose, and drench in the dew.

* * *

My friend is a one-man health. He not only owns health, but is sickened by it. It attacks him internally, and then filters out to his brain, where it converts his thoughts to worry. This is a somaticpsychlical process, which is his only claim to normality.

"How are you?" I asked my friend. (It was cruel of me, but I couldn't help it.) His answer was weird. The words were so distorted and twisted, that only a patholinguist could interpret them. I applied for an intermediate translator, but the mental institution was closed that day. (They were whitewashing the prisoners.)

My friend blames his health problem on his body. The body, its dignity lowered by its current scapegoat status, is not on speaking terms, which gives my friend frequent spells of silence. This is his contribution to the field of music.

My friend has willed his health to science. This is to go into effect the very minute he dies, so science has taken elaborate pains, on behalf of humanity, to prolong my friend's life as infinitely as possible. Recognizing its limitations, science has asked religion to help. They merged on a friendly basis, in a nonprofit arrangement disastrous to both, and are at work trying to neutralize my friend's health between an indifferent body and an indifferent soul. The result is expected to be not only spectacular, but lots of other things.

When not assailed by this dual treatment, my friend is given rest periods—for the sake of his health.

* * *

Closing the mind down on his eyes, my friend puts power into his sight, and thoughts do all his seeing. Being blind, they produce ignorance. My friend ignores this, and concentrates on his handicap.

* * *

My friend has the right to think, but the thoughts are choosy, and refuse to select him. So thinking is its own reward, for ideas know their real value, and abandon my friend at every opportunity. Some mental life still remains, and has a whole vacuum to feed on. This simplifies things.

* * *

Freedom is on my friend's mind, and thoughts find a favorable climate. He rarely disturbs them. They conduct their theories, enjoying idle and unproductive lives. My friend doesn't mind such parasites. Privileged to be intellectual, he uses them as a showcase. Without them, he hardly dares be mental. Below, his only boast is a used-up body, skin-lined, cheap, and not very permanent. The pampered ideas he supports permit his confined range of pride.

* * *

My friend's thought-filled ignorance, when applied to reading, practically empties the book of thought, and blanks out every word. If the covers are lucky, they retain the title. Fortunately, most authors are dead. They can't interfere, when my friend is intellectually molesting their books.

One day, without warning, I found my friend looking at a book. "What page are you reading?" I asked, thirsty to absorb the culture. "I won't know until I get there," he said, determined. In my younger days, knowledge was one of my ideals. "What courage," I said to myself, watching him attack the book with both eyes, "that he should want to learn in spite of all his ignorance."

Looking cautiously over his shoulder (more out of curiosity than wisdom) I noticed, to my regret, that the pages were blank. When asked to explain this, he replied, "I like to leave things up to my imagination. Self-reliance, you know."

Then he began to turn several pages at a time. "Are you in a hurry?" I asked. "Yes, my librarian gets very impatient," he remarked.

After finishing the book, he closed his eyes to think about it. "What a blank expression," I privately whispered to myself.

All of a sudden, my friend felt very ignorant. I gently escorted him to the library, and sat him down in front of an encyclopedia. "Read," I told him, and despite his weak condition he forced himself to open a volume which he read a little bit at a time until gradually his strength recuperated. "Can I go out now?" he asked me at length; "I read the whole book."

"But do you *remember* it?" I cautioned him. "I think so," he replied, and recited. The librarian heard him, and suggested he stay at table one more day with a few other books, until the danger of a relapse will have passed. The next day he was released, and celebrated by acquiring a new character trait: dogmatic conceit.

* * *

My friend tried to make a book. It was hard to write it, so he did the bookbinding first—an attractive hard cover and some empty pages blankly pregnant. The printer was getting impatient, with a squad of idle typesetters. But my friend had no inspiration; that was the trouble. Prose to him meant perfection, and anything less, according to his ideals, was imperfection. So he never wrote. The book got published, a few thousand copies, and the critics, that polite crew, blamed the style for the failure, but said nothing of the empty content. The current philosophical system, however, praised the content, and is including some passages in an anthology, the title of which is, *The Vacuum in Modern Man; Studies of our Negative Times; by Authors Addicted to the Disease of Which They Treat.* "I'm getting famous," said my friend, and before he could elaborate, a terrific yawn dislocated his jaw. "Ouch," he said, exerting his rugged realism. "There's material for your book," I warned him: "your personal experience." "Why bore the reading public?" he answered, while the sheer monotony of living drove a brutal ennui through the blank pages of his average paperback soul. My friend was so ordinary that the jaw snapped itself together again, because normality was so ingrained in its bony habit.

* * *

My friend has an extravagant affection for nothing because he likes things that are reduced to their simplest elements, by which they appeal directly to the uncluttered clarity of any comprehension. He's obsessed with Nothing, and devotes the major portion of his mind to an accurate, immediate, straight-from-life study (obstructed by no abstractions) of this fabulous, glittering phenomenon. He's an expert on Nothing, and his theories are always for sale, to the regular man in the street or to the nearest bidder. Democracy and Nothing go together, since both are ruled by the majority, and tend to be uniform throughout, through the vital process known as dwindling. Nothingness is somewhat of a religion, which my friend practices on himself, playing the dual role of clergy and layman. You should hear his soundless hymns. His after-life goal is to be admitted to Nothing, so he practices its virtues today, observing its occult rituals with a zeal so fanatic that he's already made a convert of me—in the other direction. "Believe in Nothing!" my friend requests. "Sorry, I have no faith," I tell him. Weeping like a martyr, his lips manufacture a non-prayer that speeds to Nothing. I'm not moved, and prefer my orthodox atheism, which gives vent to the pagan excess of my soul, which craves the solid nourishment of good wholesome substance. "How outrageous!" screams my friend, hysterically clinging to Nothing. I wonder what his reward will be.

My friend looked gloomy. "What's the matter?" I stooped to say. "Nothing," he answered, his voice abandoned to a disillusioned man's tone. "That's good then," I said; "or is it bad?" "I'm no theologist," answered my friend; "morality's a big question mark, and the way I see it, everything's going to Nothing." "What is Nothing?" I asked. "It's not for beauty, it's not for utility; Nothing is for its own sake." "Then why does it bother you?" I asked him. "Because I'm not sure it's complete," he replied, with the smoke pouring out of his brain. "You mean Nothing can be only partial?" I asked, astonished. The world stopped spinning, and life, for an instant, seemed but a mask-disguise that death wears to a masquerade party with the breath of midnight fading fast, at which time everything must be swept bare, and all insolent identities glaringly revealed, as the gay hour toils in triumph to its stroke.

"Then you're a Nothing fan," I said: "even though it's not pure." "Purity is scarce, these days," my friend reminded me: "thank God for a partial Nothing, or even a part-time Nothing; at least we have some Nothing, which is better than no Nothing at all." "With such wishy-washy ideals," I said, "you're hardly in a position to be a spokesman even for Nothing." "Let Nothing alone!" he retorted, and we were close to an angry fight. "What are we fighting about? Nothing!" I said, appealing to reason. "It's sacred to me!" I could hear him say, as I was falling down.

"What did you hit me with?" I enquired, for he had struck no blow, and yet a severe jolt was stunning my jaw. "Oh, only Nothing," he said—religiously. "You'll defend it to the death, won't you?" I said. "*Your* death," he replied; and then, with smug piety: "you're the unbeliever, not I." When my eyes were closed, I could see, as he had intended, that particular Nothing. It seemed like nothing at all. Yet faith has power.

* * *

My friend was almost once very smart, but recovered, or got over it, just in time to catch up with the resumption of his usual normality, which includes enough dumbness so that lapse into smartness was mercifully forgiven, if not to say outright forgotten. The grin on him is heavily weighed down by stupidity on one side and just sheer ignorance on the other, like two mediocre guardian angels over a would-be freethinker's bed, pouring loads of oblivion into the poor guy's mental sleep, so that he wakes up drugged, and doesn't know which side he has to go to the bathroom out of, and doesn't even know that he doesn't even know that he has no notion of what he doesn't know, so vast is his overwhelming lack of knowledge, nor is he faking by pretending to be modest, but he just plain doesn't know, with a clarity so real that it approaches something like purity, if purity has survived the rigors of default these days, these earth-shattering, world-violating, man-destructive days, right up until what we call now—I mean that *was* now. And so the world changes, but my friend goes on, like a tidal wave or an endless volcano, waiting the incentive to erupt. Oh, he has lava all right, enough for two lifetimes, but he keeps putting it off. "Is tomorrow okay?" he says. The thoughtless face on him, cluttered with wild orphan emotions that seem to drift or accumulate out of some generalized birthplace that no parent attended, with as much ease as the law of gravity itself, that keeps falling down all over people. So there was a grin on my friend's face, while it lasted. Which is more than you can say for most things, these days.

* * *

My friend's self-animal folded the knees and gave the behind to the seat of a chair, where the rigid comfort of sitting was established. As this occurred, my friend's mind kept looking toward an outside idea whose free life cannot be violated by physical possession. When sitting was done and standing heavily moved into being, my friend's self-animal claimed its mind, full of brain cells one of which blinked in obedience to the faraway call of that idea, whose small existence dwelled in light withdrawn from the scope of understanding or the measurement of sense.

* * *

As he started to think a thought, my friend hoped it would be deep. It was, making my friend look simple and dull by contrast, joined as he was to his skin-lined body with its evolutionary arms and legs so absurdly on a par with standard. As the thought deepened, with its weight of God, my friend continued to be identified by his regular face where, among his lips, a smile prepared its journey.

* * *

My friend had a brilliant idea. This impressed me. It reflected an immense deal of credit on his brain. But when he expressed it, it lost all value, and enjoyed but a commonplace status.

My friend blamed this devaluation on the language. "I hate English," he said. So he studied another language. He mastered it so perfectly, that there was no room left in his brain for a brilliant idea. Now he has a grudge against words. He refuses to use them. He prefers to shrug, or grunt. A new crop of ideas is growing. They show promise of future refinement.

To give them meaning, he partly hired a secretary part-time, who was so efficient that she typed his pregnant silence into eleven or fourteen distinct but brittle languages, not one of which has since or before been spoken, in the polite annuals of human intercourse where every refinement is broken up into additional refinements until ultimate coarseness is achieved, massive thick brutal stupidity, the grossest vulgarity, like the acceptable custom of eating.

Attacked by a hungry stomach, my friend employed food. With this setting, he had to eat. The meal had just finished him, and emptiness had completed the plate, when a feeling of being full occurred within my friend. Then good nothing became the best thing to do, and my friend was content.

* * *

Here's a page stolen from my friend's yet unwritten autobiography. It reveals how precociously youthful he was when he was too old to know better. His infantilism matured to an incredibly ripe regression.

"My soup sandwich dripped all over me. By the time I washed it up, the bowl was served.

"Next, I had a raisin. When it fell in my lap, my modest hostess helped me look for it. By the time we found it, she was pregnant a dozen times.

"Then, some coffee spilled. But the rug is English, and preferred tea. Realizing my mistake, I immediately dropped a muffin.

"Finally, looking in the mirror, I watched my digestion. In order to do this, I undressed.

"Weighing myself, I had lost four pounds. My hostess helped me look for them. Do you know where they were? In the bathroom.

"I reapplied them, and felt good at once. However, my friends avoided me. They held up their nose. And no wonder, because I smelled.

"My hostess put on a gas mask, and now when we kiss we don't conceive.

"Our love is so infantile, that we are the babies we make. In her maternity gown, she struggles in labor, and finally bears me. I'm reared at her breast. She gives me good cow's milk. But I homogenize it first."

* * *

Like a color-blind painter, my friend tries to live with imperfect equipment. His ears read my words out of the air, but when the words are passed to the upper brain they lose all thought in process, and drop all meaning on route. His brain signals his mouth to say something in reply. The mouth opens, and a harmless fartpuff of smoke goes forth, words that say nothing like a handsome suit in which there is no man. However, my friend has air in his lungs and blood in his veins. His life below the brain is vivid, and goes on with relentless energy.

My friend is allergic to time, and likes to turn off clocks. Some clocks, running a mile in four pulseticking minutes, slow down backwards and retreat in wild alarm when my friend puts a reactionary blockade on the racetrack of human progress. With all his living ancestors in the zoo, my friend is a living, breathing facsimile of an original inferiority complex.

Deep inside my friend are some of the most genuine emotions ever created by man's self-searching drama of the incredible. He feels these emotions with such earth-shattering ferocity, such unbelievable all-encompassing intensity, that their reality is an event that shocks the complacency of men for all time. No wonder his love scares women away, and his hate drives a spear of laughter through each fortunate enemy. If ever, in the deep beyond, my friend should have recourse to die, the explosion would sever Earth from any planetary ties, and it would wander moorless in the vacuum of eternity. Nature would cry real crocodiles at my friend's funeral, and then go off for a splashing gay holiday in the sea of indolence. And for my friend's soul, it would leap straight up and merge with the endless sun.

* * *

My friend wants to be on the good side of the sun, and he knows which side his buttock is tanned. It burns him up that the shadow he casts is his own, but it's no flesh off *his* skin. Light and heat are shed on him, and with barefaced audacity he absorbs them to the last ray or beam, naked to the consequences. He's in God's birthday suit, which recently came back from the cleaners with a stain. He calls it "my original sin," and so illuminates his origin. He uses warm terms in heatedly discussing this combustible matter, and expects hell to pay for it. He'd go up in flames, except that making an ash of himself throws damp water on his pride. So the prospect leaves him cold.

* * *

"If it isn't out of season, I must report that you seem hot," I flatly told my friend. "Seeming isn't the whole story; *is* is the rest of it," he coldly stated, as he took the ice tray from the refrigerator and swallowed the cubes one by one, and then licked the tray for good measure. "What accounted for your state?" I clinically asked. When he had refreshed himself, this, with self-humiliating deliberation, was his story, without embellishment:

"As the sun rapidly beat on the pavement, I said to my shadow, 'You lucky stiff!'

"The shadow nodded, and said with a faint smirk, 'Won't you join me?'

"I could feel my ears glow with humidity. Stifling a sweat, I violently stepped on my shadow. 'You have me pinned down,' he hollered. 'Not necessarily,' I said, ashamed of my momentary advantage.

"Meanwhile the sun stepped in, like a referee, and tugged us apart. I noticed it was August.

"The temperature followed me wherever I went. If I tried to run, it only caught up faster. So I got wise, and stood still. Then I jumped, and ran to the fire department. They trained hose and ladder on me, but the water itself was too hot. Infuriated, I waved my arms about, to divert my smoke away from my eyes. The fire, by this time, was climbing to the second of my six stories.

"A woman tried blowing a kiss, but only fanned my ardor. Luckily, a forest was not nearby. Soon, making an ash of myself, I smiled at the stake and decided to become a martyr. I was too tied up to do anything else.

"A woman enflamed my passion, depriving me of martyrdom. This burned me up."

"Your story was done to a crisp," I admired, while removing my skin preparatory to a cold shower.

Heeding my acknowledgment, my friend thrilled to a chilly shiver; the reverberation, in steady bounces, revived him beyond the state of his temperature. His survival extols insensitivity's transcendence of local flesh thermometer. What factors this removes him from!

36

* * *

My friend enjoys standing in the sun. Once he did it early in the season and absorbed so much of its fury that the sun went into a decline and set, just before evening. But it still burned in him. Later that night he passed a young flower, which, in the power of his secondary rays, grew mature at double the usual deathly pace.

When the moon came out, it glowed brighter. Why? It had to reflect my friend's stored-up heat.

Before my friend's sunburn turns to tan, can electricity be ignited from his energy bank? Better still, what are atomic possibilities?

Spies from the other side plot to kidnap my friend, while his own country claims to militarize him. The compromise is to have a Cold War surgeon carve him neutral. This partly answers the disarmament problem.

But now it's too late. He tanned and faded. Only the power to procreate remains, an issue significant only to women who allow it to concern them.

How little do we know about the sun? Our ever-breathing vitality depends on such a remote fire. My friend was blessed with inner knowledge, and now shadows degrade the memory.

* * *

"I have a complaint," issued my friend. "What is it?" I proclaimed, half in earnest jest, and the other half compounded of honesty and deceit. "It's about nature," he bemoaned, his overtime eyes working out the formula of a tear. As it fell, he glanced proudly, and closed shop. "Nature has too many leaves on trees," he catalogued, "too many grasses and flowers of the same kind, too many sons and daughters of the same animal family, too many drops of rain during one shower, too many examples of the same sample, too many copies of one edition, too many mass produced duplicates of the same manufactured article. The abundance is just too much. Why repeat a good thing, and spoil the effect of novelty? Clichés ruin the first—" "—But what of your own self?" I interrupted; "Nature began hundreds of years ago, and if it stopped after the first few humans you wouldn't even have an existence to boast of, much less a mind to criticize fertility." "But I'm fresh and original," he snapped, "I don't get repeated very often." This paltry bombast of ego made me snarl and sneer. The disgust rose to my throat, and phlegmed out on the sidewalk in a spit. "You outsized vanity of pig," I told him, while internally I disgorged a vomit's fart; "you jealous pigmy maniac, you snot-turd, you ugly ass-faced unswept manure, you seed of sterility, you pimple-cancer, you blot on the sun's record," and then, transferring this burden to my fists, I flattened him with repeated blows, to which he could only respond by falling down and sleeping on the sidewalk below him. His succession of monotonous snores made me feel sleepy and peaceful. Above, a pack of clouds paced adrift. Specks of dust, in innumerable hordes, kept middle distance in the fading of our light. Billions of windows in skyscrapers and lesser buildings ranged in geometric precision. The square of sidewalk that framed my friend was one of so many all over the city. All streets are alike, once the differences are weeded out. I began to count my thoughts. This helped me to freely associate. The last thought gave in, and feeling began. By then, a blur of confusion vaguely linked everything.

* * *

"Do you like scenery?" I asked my friend. "Not exactly," he said, "unless it's out of doors." "Yes, do you like the natural kind?" I continued to ask him. "Sure," he said; "the more the merrier." "That's fine," I told him; "keep it up."

* * *

My friend has an outdoors attitude to nature. Once I fooled him. I cut an outdoor flower off its wild natural stem and placed it inside a well cultivated vase, with the head sticking out for air. As another act of mercy, I added iodine to the water, just in case the stem where cut should have any opportunity to bleed. All was in readiness. My friend arrived. He took one look, and concluded that the room was a garden. He plugged the lawn mower into the closest socket, and shaved the hair off the rug.

Then he emptied a bag of seeds into the sink, and turned on the water to make them grow. Then he switched on the chandelier bulb, and prayed for chlorophyll. Meanwhile, he was not idle. He raked fallen newspapers, shoveled and hoed a patch of wood floor, and even squeezed a refrigerated carton until the daily ink oozed out. When the alarm clock went off, he fed it chicken feed, and told it not to crow till morn. No sooner did he do these chores, when he went behind a lamp, opened out his back face, squatted in the manner of our most primitive peasant ancestors, and produced personally his own instant fertilizer.

But I spoiled his pleasure. "This is an apartment," I told him, watching a shadow steal across his weather-beaten face. "Well ain't that so now," he said, looking about him. The window afforded our only compromise. Halfway between indoor and out, it served to remind each world about the other one without excluding either. There, suitably, was the seat of our arbitration. We sat on the sill, his feet dangling out into a rough bush, and mine in on the shaven rug. It fell to my lot to clean up dung. For his part, he agreed to forgo crops, since most of our needs were well serviced by the grocery store. I had to concede the outdoor supremacy of the sun, while he let electricity lay tame in domestic wires, the sheltered creature shedding light by the hand of science. A flower plucked out of the lap of spring is confirmed in artifice, while the table where its breath declines grew wild into a sky of rain. I sleep warm on a bed, but expect the fury of my death to romp in warm earth. Paste may preserve my teeth and lotion train my hair, but when a skeleton draws free of every civilized label, emptying the wedding ring of a well-fed finger, the stars teach bones a new dance. The rhythm will fall into the window, where my friend and I sit bargaining over the division of things. We solve a double image of a world whose beginning rages at mad odds with an incredible middle that can sprout billions of ends to divert nature and defy our practical tricks of science.

* * *

Wild spring invaded the room. "Spring is swift as God," my friend flashed. Flowers cramped the rug, choked the ceiling, electrified the walls, clogged up the plumbing, in droves and hordes, coming in forest taxis or buses from the countryside, osmosising themselves through midget window cracks and drafty door entrances, like outlawed propaganda or a clever international spy network. Flowers with exotic perfumes, moody silent ones, gay freckled extroverts, elaborate spectaculars, traditional aristocrats, humble farm types, the graceful scholars of convents, bawdy ones seen at a moment's blush, plush broad matrons, genius breeds, flushed alcoholic barflies, the society set, prisoners rotted from their cells, outstanding beauty contest winners, deep brilliants, bright captives of the sun, those in gowns of silk and those in the majesty of velvet, dignified black impoverished gentlefolk and homespun plural citizenry, the urban speedster and the rural hayseed, sweat-drenched athletes and pock-faced cripples, the chlorophyll pep fools and the casual health addicts; the spectrum catalog of complete flowerville, from paper to steel, wool to wood, outrunning native description in huge masses of assemblaged species, interflowing in freedom's wide democratic varieties, in all styles, patterns, and petals, the speckled motley of hilarious abundance overspilling pot and vase, those abounding eccentric domestics that serve the earth's surface in the lavish accoutrements of ornament, those solemn toys of festivity.

They just smothered us, yet renewed our breathing, and enriched our annual Spring supply of blood, for they were us, growing through decadence into permanence, converting the wreaths of funerals to perennial immortals, creatures of cloud and fancy, those phantoms of the earth, drunken nature, the war migrants, returning departed, the constant savages of Spring that saturate beauty with standard addicted ugliness, the drug of hope, the stray permanent exile.

"It's Spring now," my friend said, and radiated. "It had better be," I said, for seasonal economy and a harmony-ripening sense of fitness had schooled me in rigidity, and I was severely intolerant of waste. I primly added, "Every flower must count—surplus of any description enrages me." "Don't dim my joy," droned my friend, like a peaceful bee extracting the honey of paradise from the pollen-clad armpits of gigantic Creation's flower. "How sweet!" he sighed, and was now a dreamy child with curly head, pressed close in the tight hot lap of the first Mother, and nursed from the deepening streams of that serene Source. "Oh, it feels nice," he said, and fed and thirsted on all the rivers of that Sleep.

* * *

"We continually return to nature," I told my friend; "and that's a fact."
"Yes, I also like nature my own self," he genuinely replied; "it's comforting, it's life-giving. It has true value, real essence, mingled with livewire vitality, the very heart of being. It makes me feel normal, instead of out of place. It gives me a sense—" "Yes, I know exactly what you mean," I couldn't help but interrupt; "it sure is thoroughly on the satisfying side, isn't it?" So we went out, locked the safe door behind us, and cautiously approached nature. "Beautiful, absolutely beautiful," said my friend, his voice simply crawling with exquisite admiration. "I couldn't more perfectly agree with you more wholeheartedly," I ventured to inform him. Abundant ecstasy simply superswooned our total captivity, a delicious sensation of delight overwhelmed our every cell, we saw trees, grass, and clouds, and by the end we practically panicked. "Oh hold me, I'm breathless," implored my friend, and heaved into happy collapse. "Oh wonder, oh marvel," I exclaimed, and fell heavily on my back. So we were out cold, compelled in our dreamlike trance, while overhead and underground nature went right on, ignoring our approval.

We woke up, and looked around. Night was spitting rain on us, and in unhealthy dampness we gathered our energies to hustle home. "Terrific, nature," my friend once we got there said. "Most emphatically," I seconded him. We applied our towels vigorously, and with colossal appetites ventured forth on our adequate dinner. Thoughts were cruising like electricity, buzzing up and down us, the remnants of that exceptional vigor. "Boy, is nature a dynamo," I said, and shook my head from side to side with incredulity. "You're deadly right," my friend took dead aim. As a result, we fell asleep.

When morning gathered round, full of sunshine, piercing the closed windows, we felt lethargic. "Let nature alone today," my friend said, in a guilty tone. "We had better," I said; "this intensity could kill us. Let's be very tame."

So we were, and nature's ferocious wildness went unheeded. We ignored it at every turn, and wouldn't even look at the picture of a flower in a book. So with subdued hearts, and diminished vitality, we caught up with our average functioning, and were able to live more naturally.

It was a great relief, but we took it a bit matter-of-factly, by which our middle-class caution was afforded full recognition.

* * *

My friend developed a crush on nature so embracing, spring was coy and teased him by not arriving till July. And her tardy appearance came with such abrupt abundance, he was but impotently prepared, and had to dangle along platonically. So starved was he for affection, he all but bottled up the perfume of roses and violets, and then cultivated a delirium. Trees bent down to stroke him with their gentle leaves. He swooned into autumn, and grew so natural, that he claims an inhuman birth. This candidates him for religion.

* * *

One day the sky failed to appear. My friend looked at his watch. While he looked, he waited, in order to give himself something to do, like a bird that, while flying, is also flapping its wings from a busy Protestant purpose to keep high above the sinful plan of simple idleness. The weather and climate were outdoors, as nature had planned it, but the sky was remaining behind the scenes, like a bashful boxer who's trying to win the championship outside the ring, because he hates to be confined, especially with ropes on four sides and a clumsy interfering referee who pushes him and his opponent apart by style-cramping their punches with sport-defying rules and other sleeping pills, merely to promote fair play.

Without a sky, there was no sun. My friend removed his sunglasses, and took out his fair-weather eyes, with their self-regulating system of tears, that ran down from clouds of emotion that were always being saved for a rainy day, and prepared with a constant umbrella, held open like a palm extending from the alms of a beggar. "When will the sky come?" my friend's question-filled mind happened to be thinking.

So that was neither day nor night, nor the slightest degree in between. "Without a sky," my friend said, "I might as well be dead." "That's a negative way of seeing things," I corrected him, and praised the earth and sea, pointing out that they, at least, remained. "But I want the whole picture," my friend insisted, like a lover who, after finishing his woman, kills her for good measure, and then complains that she's no longer active.

Just then, like the central tenor who holds up a whole opera for vanity-suspending hours in order to set a dramatic stage, and then thrills the patience-soaked audience with the belated triumph of his appearance, the sky took place. "How complete," admired my friend, and his gratitude sprinkled the area with some high-purpose clouds, mingled throughout with the radiant effect of a sun, to give reality its most daily illusion. "At last!" he said, finishing up the touches, brilliantly imitating what, of its own course, is so regularly normal. He smiled, and estimated, after deftly fingering his pulse, that both blood and breathing were keeping an inspired rhythm together, now that harmony was restored to the highest wideness of which this world is serenely capable. "Fulfillment," he echoed, partaking of the glory. It was idle to deny him. The beauty of a completed thing. A world dream-heavened, round-realed at harmony. Let it suffice.

* * *

"Have you five senses?" I asked my friend, holding up my spread hand. He looked at it, through it, and past it. After a mental calculation, he answered solemnly, "Thousands." My sense of incredibility stood up and bowed down in amazement, after succumbing at first to an initial outburst of surprise. "In scope or intensity?" I asked him. "Both," he assured me, while a giant called Life prompted every mortal pulse of my soulbody partnership to exult and cringe with fear, pride, audacity, and a kind of melancholy joy while experience paraded past me in unending interval. "May I borrow that truth?" I asked this friend, "and apply its contents to me?" "You already have," he observed, using up thirty or so senses in so doing. I smiled, and his smile overlapped mine, while the emotion danced and twisted between us, like a trapped byproduct of two puzzled parents.

* * *

"I love the way things appear," admitted my friend, "the colors of a sunset, or the filled-in contour of a girl behind her dress. Or architecture that doesn't move, and soft water yielding to the power of a river. I love the display of merchandise in a window, and a tree turning four times around for the pleasure of a year. I love the hourly newspaper, and the book that shall never stop being read. I love the visual pre-taste of food prepared, and the empty wall of my bedroom while sleep is patient in the waiting dark. I love the memory of a dream that has just vanished, when the morning returns. I love the plain habits in sight, that simplify the sun and restore peace to the eye." "That's very nice," I replied, thinking about what he said; "but those are only appearances." "That's all I care about," he exclaimed, and closed those precious ornaments of his soul, the image-cluttered eyes, bearing all the substance he should ever know.

* * *

My eyes create sight, in the best visual tradition. For example, here's my friend, standing with his four dimensions against time and space, full of solid reluctance to yield to his inborn mortality. He has a pink skin, and words are about to emerge from his slowly opening mouth. His hands are poised in the act of raising a gesture. His feet grip our city earth, and yet their firm grace can spin the shadow of motion into any sunny interval. He stands, about to be released. His mouth smokes with a recent outburst of words, curling into the air of lost sound. Then his "goodbye" begins his removal, and now a new distance has been constructed between us. Instead of him, his image: sight converted to mind.

When my eyes see, generally color is included. Is this privilege necessary or luxurious? I don't know, but my friend has a pink face. When opened at the front, that pink face breaks out into a multiplied sound of many human words. Through that complex of words the face behind it remains almost silently pink. This simplifies the problem of seeing, but meanwhile my ears are in utter and confused misery.

"Stop talking," I tell him. His face is so surprised, it turns white, and then red. Silence is golden.

Behind the pink border of his face, the background presents a variety of characteristic colors. The famous blue of the sky. The green emblematic of nature. And the man-made colors of his abounding architecture.

After my friend dies, his pink face will be blank. Then the sky will move forward, the trees and buildings grow closer, and that former pink face will lose its ability to be seen. By that time, my eyes will be blind anyway. And meanwhile, where will pink go?

* * *

My friend has a weakness for color, and busily spends half his eyes on it, dividing and subdividing the variety-featuring spectrum into its distinct component individual colors. Nature is one source, and painting another. Colors have a tendency to combine, he found out, or coexist within a single field of harmony. Examples are found everywhere. This cultural study refines the aesthetics of his vision, and alerts his sense of sight to the laws of beauty, that have resisted change since the eyes were perfected as an evolutionary organ, in conjunction with the image-molding power of the inverted eyes developed in the highly visionary brain of man. "You like seeing, I understand," I told my friend, and he indeed agreed. To prove it, he looked. The object was a pretty woman, and his eyes were molesting her. She yelled for help, and the image of a policeman appeared in apparition. "A mirage, no doubt," scoffed my friend. The alarmed woman was in hysteric hallucination, partly due to her eyes being closed. The scene was unbelievable, and had to be seen. There was my friend laughing into the policeman's face, which was a smudge of Irish pink. The uniform was blue, leaping and twisting in the fantasy of the sun. Rough real hands grabbed my friend. I visited him in jail, which was dark, with the blind window chasing out any friendly ray. My friend's prisoner-eyes hung down, looking notoriously blank. "Was it true?" he asked.

* * *

"I'm thoroughly empty and bored," my friend announced in a swaggering tone of voice. "Well don't persecute me," I said, coming a little belatedly to my own defense. By now, our malice became apparent. Our eyes glowed with each other's defiant image, and a flow of hatred rushed panting from our panic pride of breath. However, before events got out of hand to endanger our character reputation as self-proclaimed gentlemen, a girl as soft as a rubber foam mattress happened, it chanced, to be walking by on legs so tender, the sense of feel and touch swooned into giddy lightness, and a lifetime of discipline and vigor, schooled in the patience of dignity, went mushy and crumbled into mild powder and wild, slovenly disorder, ferociously bestial and primitively crude. We oozed, sighed, and deeply inhaled. Our enmity forgiven, we became, if only for helpless mutual protection, allies to necessity and rivals by sympathy, wooing and being scorned in disastrous unrequited equality by that abrupt feminine vehicle of vanished beauty. For now she was out of sight. "Did you see that?" I asked, while my eyes were chewing the vision for memory to digest and despair to assimilate down to my most remote vessel of sorrow-soaked blood dyed and deeply tinted, to saturation, with life-absorbing love, by which the heart's overused pump grows hourly obsolete and its useful function degraded to disrepair and impoverished by neglect. "Those legs had real magic, didn't they," said my friend, and from that day on became a mystic, trading sanity for ecstasy's refined agony, and was the champion martyr of love, sainthood's heir and the crucified savior of man's bitter fall from romance. "And those tits weren't bad either," I added, in my humble earthy way.

* * *

"She knows which side she's bred to be buttocked on," I said, giving my friend a nasty wink. What a lucky dress she was wearing, to cling so softly to her closest and most intimate movements, the rich folds of her skin caressing the secret underneath of that wildly luxurious silk; and delicate sighs would emerge from the chaste negligence of their contact, the pressures and hidden kisses, a bliss formed in all the liquid flowings of touch. "I'm going mad," my friend decided, because his body was overheated. "Please do," I said, glad to be rid of a rival so unnecessary that I had no need for his presence, since that overgrown girl there smothered in the air pockets and whirlpools of her clothes, embraced by sheer products of New York City's obscene Garment Center and all the Semitic hands guilty of humid corruptions of bulky European wives, was annihilating my attention from the legal and moral foundations of my important Twentieth Century environment. "Hello, baby," I said, sucking my teeth in the wrong direction and juggling my eyes in a casual to-fro motion and crumbling my much-crumbled fingers and letting my feet hang loosely off the ground so that I tripped, sprawled, and fell, and then in the same tone of voice, "Didn't we meet before? Sure we did. How about a date." And to top it all off, I smiled, from a sitting position, revealing a self-bitten tongue and a whole mouth full of distant teeth crooked and cynical with half a lifetime of chew-biting swallowed neatly behind them and dumped down the elaborate garbage deposit of my God-endowed body, which had conceived an affectionate heat for this clothes-hugged living embodiment of a woman barely recovering from the shock of my address. "Has he molested you, lady?" I heard my friend's voice say, and knew that I had just been honored with the advent of a rival, to which my passion responded with fury and decision: "Get out of the way, you fool." Nor did he flinch. We fought. It was a manly fight. The woman shrieked, between pants of gay laughter that pierced our souls with her frank low vulgarity. "How unworthy she is," we decided. By then, we were tired. It was hard to get up.

So we lay there, we and our wounds. And then we saw some women's clothing walking away. "Was she in them?" we started to wonder, but gave up the trend of thought since the question was losing interest in us, for the fires of lust were subdued. Perhaps her clothing deserved her.

"She could wear anything. She could wear us maybe," I said, stirred to regret. It was indecent to think of her nude, so I dressed her with myself, after having been washed and dried and ironed and spotless. "Would you fit her?" my friend asked. "I don't know. What's her size?" This puzzled us. It was a long time before we dared to think again. And when we did think, at last, our thoughts were clad in the starchy linen of our restraint. An undressed woman was a mere temptress. A dressed one, surely, was the deep inspiration of the devil, molesting the imagination with a challenge of belt, buttons, zippers, hooks, catches, garters, all the tight trappings that delight to stretch heat to its stiffest nonbreakable point of ecstatic embarrassment, that incites to delinquency and enforces the prohibition of our prudence. So we put on our Sunday thoughts, and prayed to God at once. He gave us a sermon, accompanied by organ music, on the theme, "Clothes Make the Woman." We were frankly impressed. The sermon covered everything. It stripped everything bare. The body was comforting. And the end was uplifting. We were inspired out of our shoes, and naked with piety. Spirit revealed in all that flesh!

A woman was so fashionable, that even time itself was out of date, antique, old-fashioned, and so far behind itself that, despite its alert, faithful, and accurate clocks, it could never be modern enough to catch up with that right-now woman, who was really a caricature of the future and a personified forecast of what is pessimistically to come. My friend, who is out of time altogether, ignored her dress entirely, as his only interest was to get underneath up to the surface level of the skin, in order to squeeze the equality out of so superfashionable a post-woman. Which he couldn't do, for she prohibited him.

"You're beautiful," he said, as a way of getting the conversation rolling. But she only put on more clothing, and, to keep up a superior level of taste, took off an equal portion of herself, which flattered her figure front, back, and sideways, but neglected the bottom view, a lapse unforgivable in the moral sense but exciting for my friend to behold. He applauded, and called for encore. Vanity is a feminine trait, and despite being so fashionable that the future felt ancient, she performed with my friend a deed as old as humanity, and as new as the entrance of youth into the prehistoric *avant-garde* of joy's next moment before or after that stiff knockout, Now. But time, being guilty or puritanical, intervened, so that their behavior was unquestionably put to an end. The rewarded victim of this complete sequence happened, by opportunity's passing occasion, to have been what was, or is, my friend. The woman of fashion disappeared, and now only fashion is left, as well as other women, renewed by the same process that costs them the accelerated completion of their prime.

* * *

"There's a very elastic woman," my friend pointed out. "How do you know?" I said. "Stretch her and see." So I did. It was just like rubber, or a filled-in balloon. Fun, too. I never forgot it.

"Oh yes: Thank you." "That's all right," my friend said. Next day, I had no skin. "What is it, doctor?" I asked. "Why, you're rubber, man," he diagnosed. I paid him paper money. Either that, or a check stripped off me like from a pad. And then, boy, could I bounce myself!

There was no limit to my bouncing. The higher I went, the lower I came down. I studied physics that way. Not to mention astronomy, when its illegitimate brother astrology was turned the wrong way: cloud-gazing, probably. Or gathering wool from bare stars. You never know.

"Official?" I asked. "Yes," agreed the scientist. So now, when anybody doubts me, I have proof. I'm Government-certified rubber.

* * *

My friend met a girl. They overintroduced themselves so far beyond the limits of familiarity, that they ended up as natural strangers. To break the ice, he asked her what her name was. "That's a personal matter," she replied, and called him impertinent. "You take such brazen liberties!" she added with particular dignity. "Then you keep the child," my friend said, and now they never see each other except at night. He rings the doorbell, and she answers with an averted face. An invisible bed awaits them, and their postures form the shadow of an embrace, wherein neither participates. When the act overcomes them, they exchange bodies, like gift, payment, or pawn; and he departs, safely belonging to his identity, while she remains, caressed by her usual loneliness, where all her faith and power reside.

I interviewed my friend. "When you're with her, are you one?" was my first question. "Even less," he answered, and I began to subtract larger mathematics. "Describe how it goes," I said; "please!" "Very well, if you're so curious," my friend obliged: "here's how it was some-one-times, more or vaguely less," and he began, articulating with pleasure, reminiscing with pride. (My listening was all envy, and so I deliberately misheard, and the following account is distorted:)

"A grown-up girl, whose legs, in spite of walking, were being swung at the same time, moved herself on all fronts toward me. 'At last! I'm being attacked!' came the quick message I flashed for myself; and I began to try to learn how to know to be prepared. Too late, and by now, by penetrating my defense, the girl had converted it to offense, in the twinkling of an instinct. My body found this uncomfortable, and rushed out through one exit. The mob scene nearly broke the door down, and later fire was declared, to make it seem all an accident. Smoke was ushered forth, rolled on to stage, and puffed up out of proportion. A visiting fireman took a telltale photo, but only the negative was released. By then, the girl had escaped through her most remote disguises, and appeared to me clad in a new identity. As a familiar stranger, she gained access to an old nostalgia, and this weakness fortified her re-admission. We voyeured ourselves, thrilled in the crowd of being alone."

Here's how I really pictured it, inserting undress and the clothing of death onto the shocking scene, exposed and portrayed by my unrelenting sense of imagination, by whose courtesy I gained vicarious access, and felt every inch like my friend, especially the short crucial inches hidden beneath the partner's skin and enclosed with smothering warmth until squeezed and reduced, squirting itself free, like a soul that slips off a discarded body and vacates the eternity that only sensation could provide, and begins its chaste wandering far from the body-tormented earth where its fierce boldest pleasures reigned:

A girl sexitized my friend, causing him not to find his clothing until they were lost. He undressed from nudity to nakedness, and then stripped himself. She, meanwhile, was camouflaged into, through, and between the bed. Nothing separated them but hair and skin. They wore each other for clothing, until the rips and patches showed through. Then they sewed, but the thread and needle went the wrong way, and they were swallowed into one and the same person, with a texture indifferent to weather, a mind far too patient for seasons, and a functional form far in advance of gender. They merged into general air, or practical nothingness. After their heat was spilled, an anaesthetic numbness controlled all sensations, magnetized from afar by the dim needle of death.

"Sex causes us to die," I told my friend. "That's not nice," he answered. "What's not? Sex?" "No. To die." "Oh. But then you wake up again, don't you?" "How can I tell? There are all ways of waking up," said my friend, as the sheer drowsiness of my company kept his eyes closing more than opening, and a spell of dozing stole him from this morbid obscenity I doted upon with profane philosophical compulsion, matching fears and desires with glee and gloom. Hark now. My friend awakes.

"Is it any time?" he asked. "It's always some time," I replied. No comment from him. I needed him to speak. First would I prompt him. "When you wake up in the morning," I began, "is it a real wakening, or just an official act to draw a ritual between night and day?" "It differs," my friend replied; "but once I woke up with such optimistic vitality I almost couldn't believe it. My vigor was actually transcendental, as though God in triumph had advocated the dawn and was sponsoring my flesh. It reminds me of a story: No, it happened to *me*." "If your revelation is astonishing, tell it unhesitatingly," I implored, and was gratified with this instantaneous burst of compliance:

"I woke up feeling too good to be true. That was my first mistake.

"I yawned, and with powerful ease of breath blew the ceiling away from my bedroom, until the lady upstairs fell on me with violent curiosity of desire.

"I married her next day to facilitate our growing friendship. It was a marriage of convenience, since she was intolerably wealthy and I was sufficiently poor.

"She made me move upstairs. We cooked our meals by rubbing our bodies together while holding the raw meat and vegetables. It was amazingly effective. Animal heat, as yet unexploited, contains unlimited possibilities as a source of energy. We thought of selling ourselves to the government: But that would be prostitution.

"This story ends, though, sadly: We loved each other to extinction. Even our graves are invisible."

* * *

My friend puts off shaving till the last minute, well aware that as soon as he finishes, the face hair will make a comeback in the do-or-die spirit of never-give-up. So he waits. The beard is prolonged. Suspense builds up, shadows creep across his face, the razor is uneasy in his hand. Agony and drama. He seizes the hour of twilight, covered up by the hush of surprise, and then—attack! It's a bloody contest. But the hairs are annihilated, vowing to return. My friend is bloody, but unbowed. To the victor, his own triumph.

With such a clean face, what should he want to do but get kissed? A date has been prearranged. Darkness. They hold hands. Action. They kiss. Blood, blush, and lipstick. Is my friend red!

But he's a manly man. He came out of boyhood—the best sort of training—and now his sex is so male, his gender so pronounced in a lopsided, vicious proclamation of itself, that women are afraid to walk the street at night and remain kneeling at the side of their bed in increased religious fervor. A few become martyrs, and surrender at full length to my friend. Their flesh is so devoured, the spirit has no strength to assume the ardor of sainthood, and so that too is sacrificed to the endless male ego of my all-consuming friend.

By then, it's time to shave again. He eyes the mirror, scowls, and slits his face, scaring the hair into hiding. The gods are thirsty, and his blood feud rips along, and chunks of his beautiful beef are carved into hell—where fallen women, starved for ages, tear up the vital matter and gorge their bellies full, and their harsh shrieks bounce off the planets and become the mating roar of any slovenly beast that roams the foul cycles of this bitter lust. My rotting friend resumes his brute self. Death is buried, survived by the male. The millionth face of my friend stands out for the world to see. The features are sharpened, and fate beware.

After having shaved, my friend is a clean-shaven animal. Animal? That's putting it mildly. That's a fig-leaf euphemism, considering what my friend is in becoming, at the barest and least minimum presence of a girl over the age of two and under the maximum age of compulsory retirement, because the stimulation that ensues needs a billion whitewashing censors to even modify the toning down of it, so excessively non-passive are my friend's power-packed glands and atomically nuclear set of stupendous genitals, ready at any time to divide the multiplication of our already additionally subtracted universe, that he would people with himself so many times over as to project his immortality into the never-ending future and even make God jealous. But wait, religion comes later. But not much later. It follows, because guilt is in proportion to the capacity for intensive pleasure and delightfully remarkably greatly terrifically rewardingly astonishingly terribly beautifully immaculately deeply preponderously stupendously magnificently absolutely—I don't know what. But it must be something. Otherwise, why all the fuss?

When there's a girl handy, my friend gets all fouled up with what goes for instinct, if such a thing can be said to exist in so animal-like a person, full of barbaric tendencies and pre-tribal inclinations like that ravishing sexpot, the amoeba, who makes love inside his own house to his friendly neighbor, himself—or itself, rather. Deep inside him, where it really counts, and only essence dwells, my friend is a complete brute. He even thinks like one.

So when a girl is handy, my friend, impelled by something wilder than instinct, something far cruder and more primitive than the need to survive, goes nuts, goes flat bottom nuts. He's no longer any man, not even a drive, and even biology refuses to be responsible, and as for chemistry, it prefers the laboratory, thank you. Only metaphysics can account for it.

He sizes up his prey, with those squinting things he uses which in real life are just seeing-dog hormones, and the drip goes out of his fangs full of purple greed and the green venom of sin, and now if lust never existed before—if it just walked on earth full of early innocence—it gravitates like destiny where nature places it in the supreme order of logic, dropping it dead center into theology's most abstract hell, better known as the flaming organ of my friend—who, incidentally, is just a passive observer of this surgical violation of cosmic ethics—a bystander, you might say. At this point, the girl has narrowly made her escape. She has fled, leaving my friend to hold his bulging bag full of unnecessary energy. "What should I do with this?" he asks me. I look the other way, not wishing to spoil my appetite. "Have you thought of reproduction?" I ask him—a textbook term I had once learned. "What's that?" he wondered, and I laughed to see his brain amid such stubborn flesh, like a tiny marble glittering between the bulky folds of a mammoth football tackle. But as for the task at hand, I told him what reproduction meant, and how it was indirectly responsible for the outsized population ratio, using birth as the primary vehicle. My friend was fascinated, and lapped up these facts hungrily, like a young dog straining for his graduation exercises to become a full-fledged stud-horse, and taught to pant like a ready-made stallion, a mare being in view, and salivating to the ding dong of that most celebrated of all bells, good old conditioned reflex, enabling anyone with enough sense to go literally to the dogs. "I love reproduction!" my friend announced, and went out in search of a partner with whom he might generously share his new scientific crime. I wished him luck, and sighed. "Dear me, what a most unusual world we live in," I said to myself, and nearly died of the surprise. Hours later, my friend came back. He had lost weight. "Have you eaten of the apple?" I asked, quoting at large from some biblical source. Of course he didn't understand, so all night we stayed up learning the bible, which confused his sexuality no end. "I'll be a priest then," he announced, while dawn was tuning up in a little bird's throat. "You're addicted to extremes," I said. This flattered him, his vanity was so tickled that when he began laughing I knew that it would be several centuries, before inertia would prevail on him, for decorum's sake, to stop. Now I hardly listen, except when a sudden urge for amusement relaxes my ear control, and then those consecutive peals of laughter, expressing sin and guilt and atonement, come rushing in like the march of the Crusaders, the stealth of missionaries, the public alarm of the evangelist, the mummified secrecy of the nun, the rigid cynicism of the movie censor; and strict prudent prohibition everywhere. A foul, wise laughter, that penetrates the normal waking nightmare and violates the purity of a peaceful spring day, with its harsh accents of religion and violent beats from the first drum of the archaic savage beast, who toils his squat arms in a dirty low sun. A chant, mingling prayer and marriage, lends its accompaniment, an echo doomed to fulfill the human race.

* * *

A policeman, in every sense of the law, arrested my friend for being illegal. "How does it feel, now that you're a sinner?" I asked (during visiting hours, of course). "My conscience isn't pleased," he remarked, while devils sizzled and crackled (my good ear is tuned to hell). I gave him a new fig leaf to turn over, and he undressed it on, while I admired the sunset of his blush. "What had you done?" I innocently asked, turning my cheek the other way. "I hit a girl," he confessed, in blood-colored words. "How foul!" I jolted, like a knight who just fell off his horse; "Why, in the world, why?" The formation of a tear appeared, but then his eye blinked it away. "She had a period," he said, "just at the wrong time." I practically tilted in a speechless fury, and a screech of indignant womanhood dimmed my morbid sense. My manly defense of the helpless sex arose with wrath, lending moral courage, and I struck him a blow that rang in pealing tones through his well-deserved cell. He collapsed, bruised in soul as well as crushed in body. I stalked out like a hero, passing the amazed guard. With slow deliberation, I unclenched either fist, and while pausing for a fresh release of breath, I suddenly wondered, "Why didn't I get her phone number?" About to turn back, I hesitated in a twinge of balance, shrugged, and sadly continued on my way.

Nevertheless, I had the urge to sin. When released from jail, my friend would become handy. He, I decided, would atone for everything within my unrestricted license that audacity and pleasure drove me to do, commit, indulge, make, and misbehave about, so I rubbed my palms together, and drooled in the gloating privilege and freedom from restraint that arranged my foul delights with great management and order, so that they should achieve maximum execution.

After self-indulging a few of my favorite appetites, I assigned my guilt to my friend, whom I appointed in my stead as a target for outraged Conscience. I knew I was evil and sinful every time I heard him say "ouch." While contemplating new evils and sins, I noticed my friend sweating as though a couple of up-to-date crucifixions had rented out his interior for their blood-letting occasions of honor and atonement, while he, as proprietor, feared an honest fire and a damned reputation of ill fame for his establishment, for God was rumored to be one of the spectators. He asked me to control my flesh, or at least to subdue the lusty impressions on my mind, where my behavior found such responsible origin. "Please," he begged, and made the sign of the halo. Then piety swept over me. "I promise," I wept, and vowed to do my best. I enlisted the aid of willpower. My friend was pacified. "Expect a lapse or two in the beginning," he cheerfully warned, "and then counterattack with all your noble strength. You'll improve as you get better. But make sure not to fall in love with willpower. That's vanity too, and as a reaction you may lose all you stood to gain." Splattering tears all over him, I thanked him joyfully, while praying for an unlikely miracle. Nothing less would serve me.

To repair a breach of modesty, as well as to pacify my tyrannic prudishness, I let a week slip by without letting nature drag me to the bathroom. Like barbells improve muscles, this strengthened my willpower. Soon my willpower towered high above me, as the eye of a painter will outdistance his other faculties, or the ear of a violinist will grow to the size of an elephant. If I tried to pour the sauce of pleasure over my food, willpower would swipe the plate away and feed voluntary starvation to all my captive taste buds. Or if I thought sleep luxurious, willpower would poke my eye awake and trip up my yawn till it fell flat on a sigh. And if a girlfriend ran me backwards into chasing her, until the agony of suspense provoked her to yield up her surprise under the confidence of her dress, willpower, like a totalitarian fire engine, rescued me from the blaze.

But when I began to enjoy willpower, and took pleasure in curtailing any wayward sense, and loved the daily role of my self-martyrdom—then the rigorous system of control collapsed internally. Like the air oozing out of a punctured balloon, or middle age muscles drooping on an ex-weightlifter, my willpower decayed an overnight death, leaving only my conscience as arbitrator between desire and delight. Then I arranged to sleep so long, that nature was recuperated. I woke up in excellent humor, and rained my solid and liquid waste in vengeful torrents down the churchlike sanctity of my toilet. Next, it was time to deal with my stomach. This organ of mine, once the pampered favorite, was now as prodigiously empty as the bag of Santa Claus in the eyes of a disappointed poor child. I filled it up so bulging, that farts were rushing out all over me, and burps issuing from my tonsils. The food ran down my digestion in shifts, like factory workers during a production crisis of full overtime. Assimilation was slow and treacherous, and my heart in alarm pumped out so many gallons of blood that Red Cross spies kept broadcasting donation appeals from the loudspeakers concealed within their nonprofit ambulances. After I had filled my belly, and eaten to satiety, I lifted my napkin to my chin, and wiped away some extra cattle that were lingering there. Then lust seized my groin. I phoned my girlfriend. So impatient was I, that I used the phone in her own bedroom. Since there was no extension, and I was hogging the wire, she kept getting a busy signal, so to avoid red tape she answered in person: "Hello, who's this?" Meanwhile my groin kept pumping saliva into my loins, and nature's secretions were so fertile that I grew a sudden erection which involuntarily knocked over the grand piano. The noise interrupted the telephone conversation. Of a musical turn, she went to tend to the piano. I helped her. We fell inside, and our music was like a beast with two Bachs. Between movements, I lost her. "Where are you Haydn?" I called. As I Raveled the chords, she disclosed her identity. "Are you able to Handel me?" she teased. Striking on a theme with variations, we played a fugue. As the climax squeaked, I called her "my organ grinder." Her only reply was to give birth to a baby grand piano, and this note brought down my silence all over the stage. In homage to that great virtuoso, myself. Awed by my power, I retired, and sought my friend. I had performed, and the performance had been slightly too much in excess of the normal cultural budget of the individual's aesthetic capacity for the admiration of the beautiful in sensual overtones to the tune of private pleasure, penalizing willpower abundantly. I had overdone it, and my friend's conscience was prepared to quite haunt me out of my pants. How would the scoundrel utilize that advantage? I must placate him, and at the same time console my dignity. Ah, the sweet flower of guilt, planted by seeds of violence. Prick me, thorn. I reek of its perfume. Leaf me alone, for I stem from the earth. Where, I'm told, forgiveness dwells.

Ashamed of my excess, I sought out my friend. "Now I'm dead," he said, and practically died. "I forgot you," I moaned; "you were my conscience. Did it nag you?" "Nag! I'm dead, I tell you. You sure are a beast." "It's my humanity," I pleaded. "If that's humanity," he said, referring to my recent immorality, "then what would you have not done if you had just been an animal?" "That remains to be seen," I said, and looked forward to it, with a trinkle of pleasure darting forth from my nether eye, while white glue and other leaks floamed gloriously from my assortment of outlets. "You're not only human," observed my friend, "but you're even more so." "Stop defining me," I snapped: "I defy it." In disgust, my friend walked away.

"Wait, I want to give you a present," and I ran after him: "It's a baby grand piano, play on it all you like. It's brand new, we just made it." "I'm not musical," bluntly replied my friend, and to resist temptation he put a fig leaf on each ear. This did not impede, however, the strong rhythmic beats, performed by the composer, Nature, within the concerted hell of his own private concert hall, where he had the honor of a season's subscription and had to remain sitting quietly while the music rose to its crescendo. "I can't stand it, I hate restraint!" my friend screamed above himself, slamming his willpower aside, and attacking the grand piano in the direct, grand manner. He produced an incredible range of notes on a vigorous scale, like a prisoner just released from abstinence and going on a big binge. The piano flatly collapsed, and proved hollow inside, with a thud. My friend went right on playing, for he was inspired. He displayed abandon, in high and deep furioso, in the impetuous manner. Paganini would blush, and even Nero douse water on himself. And they aren't used to second fiddle, either. My friend literally had to be restrained. In gorgeous heroics, he wept. He poured out the hysterics, and went wild. Poor slob. Some pleasure is deserved, but all pleasure is punished. The dull ache or the sweet agony, remorse kills you. I stood aside, and watched him suffer. Myself, I felt free again.

* * *

"Can't I do *anything*," despaired my friend, "without my conscience stepping in like a congressional investigating committee?" "Why? Doesn't your conscience like women?" I asked him, moderating my smile with a tug of heartfelt sympathy. Plunging headlong into philosophy, with neither a map nor a dictionary, my friend summed up life: "It's hell," he said. "Don't jump at conclusions," I warned him, "before the egg is hatched." "I'm no farmer," he said, "that I have to worry how to feed the world with agriculture." Returning to his complaint, I brought up the conscience again. "Just how does it operate," I asked him: "by what mechanical principle?" "Let me illustrate," he said, with the patience of a Job or a Freud: "Last night, out late with a girl, it came to kissing time. I rubbed scented vaseline onto my lips, secreted paste over my teeth from an internal cleanser, filled up the pores of my tongue with distilled droplets of high-powered mint, and anti-salivated the mouth wash in a thorough gleam of transferable hygiene. Synchronizing the kiss with our clicking heart-watches until the perfect second was timed to the ripest practical fulfillment, we overstepped the boundary and fell facelong down the ancient corridor of wicked Mother Lust." "Go ahead," I yelled, feigning mild indifference. "Well, when we finished our pleasure and put away our instruments," he informed me, "Conscience arrived on the scene shouting 'Am I late, am I late?' Before I could answer, Conscience extracted the truth from the guilt-ridden air, and assigned me to this Limbo of punishment: For future, after I roll myself into my contraceptive prior to use, the girl must write legibly on the business end, 'This is wrong,' with a mascara pencil. Then, after signing it, we will feel separated by this thin document, despite our efforts to come together." "Will you break your contract?" I asked. "I wouldn't have a kid on my conscience," he replied.

* * *

"What are you doing with three kittens?" I asked my friend. They were peeking out from his pockets, besides picking them. "They're the products of an overcured conscience," my friend was happy to announce, and slipped me three paternal cigars, already well lit. "Explain all this," I said. "Well it all began with a kiss. Should I continue?" "By all means."

"I kissed a girl but my conscience, like a contraceptive, prevented true contact. 'I'm a dog with a muzzle,' I thought, and went around the corner to drop into the psychology store. 'What can I do for you,' the clerk said, looking at me very intently. Before I could reply, he added, 'That will be ten dollars, please.' I paid him and walked straight out, with a great burden off my chest, a load of conflict off my mind, and a genuine catharsis in my wallet. I tried kissing the same girl. That night, she conceived three kittens."

We celebrated, of course, by drinking, after the cigars were devoured. Their mother had vanished, but the three kittens sipped their quiet milk from a liberal ash tray. My friend loved to solve multi-purposes. His kiss was packed with a lethally explosive virility.

* * *

Hired by my conscience as its spy and sly salesman, my friend helped to expose my vulnerable defenses, though pretending an alliance with me. He knew how my guilt could declare itself.

With earnest assault, conscience cracked down. "But I haven't done anything yet," I reprimanded. "Don't worry, you will," came the well-fed purr. Undaunted, I went out and committed. "Didn't I tell you," conscience wheezed. "But you didn't say not to," I defended. Thus well upholstered, I engaged my friend. "How's your conscience these days," he gaily cracked. "Oh I have him well under control," I said; "he's behaving." "Does he let you be?" my friend demanded. "As much as I want: my conscience is like a reformed parent; his way of thinking, after years of education, has come around to tolerate mine." "Then you're free!" he declared with a scorn of envy. "Free?" After crossing my fingers and knocking on the nearest sacred wood, I replied, like an undergraduate monk in a municipal monastery, cooled in the baptism of his pious sweat, "How can I dare to be?" Treated to his smirk, I lowered my pale head. Internally, my conscience was having a New Year's Eve party, getting drunker by the minute and dancing obscenely with a girl whose frequent thighs indulged my timid fantasy to the breaking point.

My friend left me. His assistance in my self-destruction could create a redundance and an interfering reversal; so this skilled agent let nature's disease soil the sex-rankling soul.

* * *

Sleep softened my friend's head, and a female dream came to life. She waved her beauty in the deep wish of his eyes, but sleep was a gentle prison and kept that wonder love from bursting free.

Inside of his mind, my friend was consoled by hope against inadequacies outside. Thought made a fantasy that reality had no admission to violate. A woman without breath or blood dwelled in my friend's mental life, and achieved existence by being beautifully nothing. To give her substance, my friend grew a ready soul of love which he soon became, and now the woman was real.

My friend wrote a letter to his girlfriend. He never met her, but at least the letter was real. She was a love-coated image. Halfway through the letter, my friend had to stop. The teardrops were blurring the ink, interfering with the romantic words that gushed from his dripping heart. The style was sheer sentiment, punctuated by pure sighs in love's own grammar. So touching was it, my friend tried suicide with the pen, but only stained his shirt near his practically breaking heart. The letter remains unmailed, waiting for the magic girl to appear in the waves of the wind and sun, and in the holy transforming moon; whose rare soulful beauty is worthy of my friend's tragically poetic love, by all that is great and divine on the shallow surface of this infinity that bears the enriched pettiness of our existence.

Oh, love love love. Oh, love. Oh, it's so deep. It became a specific girl, whether living or dead, faked or imagined, true or less, in the many-sided estimate of existence. Her body was dubious, or doubtful at most, but she must have had a soul because my friend wasn't in love for nothing, you bet. He's a realist. Take my fact for it.

My friend was in love. He did lots of sighing, and the air nearby turned sickly yellow. Unable to produce tears, he cried with dry despair. His blood refused to flow, settled into lumps, and left the skin whitely abandoned, full of imagined illness and the dull throbbing of a vacant brain. "This is serious," he managed to say. Day by night, cruising throughout his forlorn body, the wasted image of a girl was lit by a poor central candle whose rays shed blindness for the sad internal eyes. "I love her," were his swoon words. "Love," his ghost repeated. "You're early!" he said, addressing his ghost. "You're a thousand years old," answered that invisible creature, "and your ripeness is mellow. Are you ready?" "Wait," my friend implored. "For what?" asked the ghost, who, except that he had no qualified lips, might have spread a smile over the features he lacked. "For her," my friend wanted to say, but instead a moan came out of his mouth like a cry of earth. "Stop imitating me," the ghost objected, but anger caused him to vanish. The thick odor of solitude remained. Then, emerging from a dream, the girl herself began to appear, her space solid and her time instant. "Are you real?" my friend was able to say. "Try holding me, and see," teased the image. "Then I won't try," answered my friend, "if you'll be kind to stay." There was no reply, only blindness wrestling with love, and the girl's silhouette charming the air, smothering beauty with her absence. Sight escorted a wealth of tears from the blind man's eyes, the wettest actual thing he could feel. All else was hiding, or had forfeited existence.

* * *

I forced my friend to confess that he was in love. "Is she quite special?" I asked. He fainted with affirmation. "Go into detail: what's she like?" I demanded. After thinking, he produced this description (It had at least poetic truth, although entitled *Portrait of Far More than a Lady*. One thing my friend never did was to exaggerate. He didn't believe in it. All he did was distort the truth, and make a lie altogether. But this description is accurate.):

"She's so clean that she only takes a bath for exercise. When she emerges from the bathtub, the water is as clean as when first issued from the mint. Her teeth are constructed of permanent toothpaste. Her breath is so fresh, you feel like slapping her. Her eyes are so quick, the lens hands a fast print of the image to the retina before the very event on which the image is based has even been allowed to take place. Her kiss is so effective, pregnancy awaits no further cue. And when she smiles, the sun, outdone, hides behind a baser cloud.

"Wherever she walks, men cling to each toestep, and hide in the cloak of her private shadow. Any word she speaks automatically changes the dictionary. A sentence is liable to start a new literary movement. And with each paragraph, the language has changed from archaic to modern.

"If she so much as sails on a ship, the whole ocean, from mermaid to shark, becomes an exclusive pond, and the waves vie against each other to escort her to safety. A hurricane doesn't even dare sneeze.

"I touched her once, and made her autograph my finger. Then I bought a glass case for that finger, and haven't used it since.

"She has never perspired a day in her life. Her nights I can't be too sure about.

"Whatever faults she has are blessings. And her virtues have already exposed Heaven for being a fraud.

"And as she enters an empty tub, the bath fills with original water. Life's source, she creates. Beauty's outstanding myth."

"If she's so mythological, can your love have a real basis?" I categorized. "Love *lives* on the unreal," he replied grimly, sighing for that particular goddess in which he deposited the embroidered treasures of his fantasy, devotion, adoration, loyalty, respect, admiration, irrational esteem, fidelity, and other bonds that emotively sign the soul's allegiance. "Is she worth all that?" I began to ask. He didn't let me finish, and intercepted my doubt. His conviction was so firm, I mercifully didn't puff it away. The elaborate shell that housed the snail of love did its dark, protective job.

* * *

My friend and I were rivals, but for different girls. After both losing we made up, patted each other respectively on the other back, and offered each other an exchange of losses for the sake of sharing. This repaired damages to the heart, by airing out the laundry of one's personal loneliness and letting the other one whiff the odor as it dries in the same sun. We pooled our sobs and swam in them knee deep, to avoid mass drowning. This buoyed up our sagging spirits, anchored in the mud of grief.

* * *

"Have you any spare feelings?" I asked, looking for a handout. "Sorry, I used mine all up," lied my cheaphearted friend; "why? are you broke?"

"Yes, I have a broken heart, but there's no pain to go with it." "Maybe she was ugly?" he declared. "That's funny, she was," I realized, and pop!—my heart was whole.

* * *

Scenting, in my friend's vicinity, some pent-up salty moisture, I sent him a vent by way of a compassionate quiz.

"When you're not using them," I probed casually, "where do you usually keep your feelings?" "In my heart," he answered gently, and I, confessedly, was deeply touched. "And they're safe there?" I warned. "I never let women in," he said, and then added, cautiously, "if I can help it." "But if she sneaks in the back way?" I dared to suggest. "I'm only human," he confessed, and proceeded, after a pause for reflex, to weep.

Then dwindling to a drizzle and left to their own device, the tears contrived to stop. When his eyes had dried, I delicately asked, "And who was she?" "Is," he admitted, winked briefly, stepped away, and watched the torrent fall.

The splash on my shoes formed a rainbow image of her. But before my friend could pluck the bubble, it dispersed in a burst. He remained in that stooping posture, his fingers open on the gushing emptiness.

* * *

"Ever in love?" I mentioned to my friend. Then, when his smile stopped hurting, his answer hung on his voice before his tone came into certain evidence: "Funny you should ask, but I was just dreaming the same thing myself."

While the subject was being changed, a drop from his drenched private heart assured me of his tears. All the while, a terrible dryness guarded his eyes, like the hasty Holland thumb that saves a nation from its dike.

"If I touch him," I thought, "his past might turn inside out, and a woman step down from her image into fact."

So I increased our distance, like a dancer walking backward off the cliff, until our friendship was out of sight in the intervening silence of a year.

Tapped without warning on the back, I turned full scale around and saw the wholesome remembrance of my friend. "What were you doing all year?" I uttered to my surprise. Equally taken aback, he spread his shoulders in a grumbling way, leaving his hands outstretched to demonstrate a point. His face wore his expression without much confidence, but meanwhile health peeped out from his body, like the muscles independent of their athlete. "You're fit, you're in shape," I articulated, as though indifference had just given birth to an admiration. After a quite automatic thank-you, he shaped a pleasant smile on his mouth, keeping it there as long as psychology required.

When the smile had worn out its comfort, the face was pulled in by a sag, while the eyes evened out in their sockets and searched for breath. "About love," he reminded me, "I thought about it, every day. The emotion was gone a long time, but the thought remained like the tree in winter. My mind outlined her, but the body had no more juice in it, and she was blank in the face, like a doll without eyes."

I thought this quite remarkable. Here he was confessing. I encouraged it.

"When I lost her," he went on, "it was like I didn't know where to look for myself, and even the mirror was hiding the secret. Of course, she didn't exist. Or I mean she turned over her existence to my feelings and then dropped out of sight so that her absence could feed my feelings fat and dizzy. But then when my feelings disappeared, only my thought was left. Since my thought didn't have any more meat on it, now I'm beginning to forget."

I felt like taking notes, but the speech was over. He trembled a little as he spoke, which gave his words some smack, or authority. His sincerity made me nervous, but at the same time I was grateful. It saved me from reading a novel. It was the same thing, only slightly less literary.

After I thanked him, we walked on together. Before the hostility had grown too marked, we gave each other a hasty goodbye, while he retreated into memory, and I staggered into fact.

* * *

My friend was about to alter his whole face, and rearrange the muscular controls behind it, in order to serenely concentrate on the construction of one well-rendered smile. But before he could put through this act and notify the face of the change it could expect to receive, a surge of sadness gained access to every gateway of expression. The blood drooped out of him, and he was now the enactment of a long pale sag. "Well done," I applauded, like a veteran theatergoer with a taste for supernatural realism, whose highly refined boredom can be subdued by a forceful show of drama that makes the world turn artificial before stagestruck genuinity. But my friend was now so sad, real pity was expected of me, and art had to be laid aside for a glibber hour. His eyes dried up with non-tears more eloquent than the watery stuff. His downcast mouth played a dumb barrier to the mute words. "Did you lose love?" I asked.

When he said yes, I saw a universal truth, billions of losers dead and living, giving poetry its heart and music its agony.

* * *

My friend was sobbing, and I felt sorry for him. I held a handkerchief under his nose, and with the dry part I cleaned up his eyes. His spasms began to sink back in him, and the trembling breast withheld its harsh beat and then resumed a calmer rhythm. The clouds vacated his face, and left an uncertain smile standing there like a chick just out of egg. A ray beamed in his eye. A clean stream of breath flowed back and forth in his highly efficient, germ-free nose. Teeth came out of doors, and the tongue dipped back in to stir up the word stew that was quickly heating. In fact, he became overcured. I felt weak in his strength.

What could I do but weep? But the handkerchief he applied was so damp, the pity was slobbering all over me, like a romantic poet going sentimentally insane. "Control yourself," he said. Applying this advice, I was cured. This weakened him. "Don't!" I warned; "the handkerchief is too wet."

He swallowed back potentially thousands of words, and added that he was shy. "Let's all be very humble today," I suggested, speaking for myself as well. Life had put us on earth, but the strength of events was our complete master, providing our inadequacy with the dreary round of proof. "Go easy," I said. "Slower the better," he understood. Like frail lions exposed to hearty Christians in a barbaric Roman arena, we fought a losing battle against the dizzy delicacy of nerves prone to the vicious assault of sense. He tilted on one side, I on the other, displaying battered bodies and crumbled, overused hearts, and a pair of memories that demanded the most vivid barricades of repression. "Don't cry," I said; "can't you laugh instead?" "I'd rather be stiff, or safe and numb," my sad friend said, "and God protect us against being active." "Shall we share our pity?" I wondered. "Oh let's," he agreed, and a blaze of eagerness flashed momentary heroism in those long-suffering eyes. "This mighty skin," I said, "is worn by the wrong customers, us. Let's abandon the fight, retreat from glory, and give up the ground to worthier competitors." "You mean to grass and flowers,' my nature-loving friend remarked.

"And what of love?" I reminded him. "That," he said, "is a subject that may best be buried, and retired from the stings of contemplation and from talk's agreeable social tortures. Peace is not yet." "A few small more years like this," I said, looking ahead, "and though our endurance gets thinner, a comfortable end approaches." "Bliss and sweet reward," squealed out my friend, behind eyes with their squinted, inverted light reserved to console the embittered patience of a worldly martyr.

"God," I said, beginning to cry; "we are weary. Come rescue us." "That goes for me too," added in my friend, and our crooked, twisted prayer feebly attempted to fly. It crashed, emitting a tiny noise, such as only insects are equipped to hear. We stood by, protesting our innocence, the joint authors of every conceivable mold of futility that ever punished effort and grew juicy ripe fruitlessness on a tree of agony in the season of constant pain.

"We should sell our tears," I remarked, for we were poor. "What, and flood the market!" rejoined my friend, who had always been a frustrated economist in his spare time, which, considering his unemployment, was around the clock. "The supply and demand would make another Noah's ark out of us," he added in a rare triumph of sarcasm. "You mean we had to sail before?" I asked. "That's right, and bear all evolution on our backs," he consented, while man's racial past and dim origin applied new torment and further grievance to his poor, tattered reflection, and gloomed him to the burden of worry. "You're Jesus!" I declared. "But watered down," he emphasized, sprouting new tears on a faded face worn away to sand almost by the friction of life's sadism.

"Take it easy, you're killing yourself," I cautioned, with true alarm and an apprehension of dread. "Thank you," he replied: "I'm not very good at anything else." "Are you a defeatist?" I asked. "No, defeated already," he said, and his crippled unhappiness had to resort to the crutches of a smile, but the crutches themselves were unhealthy and noticeably limped, completing this serene scene of life's typical hell.

* * *

"Why are you crying?" I asked my friend. "I'm not, you are," he observed, perhaps too sharply. Yes, the tears were mine. "Why make a scapegoat of me?" I asked, tears turning to defiance. He blew my nose into a hand-kerchief, and wiped my eyes dry. "Feel better now?" I asked, my voice simply aching with pity, while I gently stroked his cheek with a furious, violent blow of my fist. "That didn't hurt, did it?" he wanted to know, as my humility suffered me to turn the other cheek.

* * *

My friend was laughing one day, and precisely because nothing was funny. He exhausted his laughter. He took a glass of water, sighed, hiccupped, and grew a grim face. Indeed, he had been laughing for thirty-four minutes straight, certainly a record. During that period, he had not interrupted himself once: just straight, continuous laughter, without inflection, steady as death, and just as humorless. This was an ordeal.

He needed a long rest. But just then, a lot of funny things happened. As illustration, a man tripped on a banana peel, and wound up eating it. Item: A lady crossed the street, having forgotten to take along her legs. They were standing on the sidewalk all by themselves. Powerless to *run* after them, she had to meticulously avoid traffic, but when she got back at the risk of her life the legs disowned her. Thus faced with a disastrous loss of sex appeal, she stumps about like a politician.

Anyway, funny things like this were happening. And right in front of my friend's eyes, too. For example, an airplane collapsed in midair, right near a handy cloud, so the pilot jumped onto it and was transformed on the spot to a heavy white angel, in clear view of the fire department below, whose impotent hoses belched hellfire and snarled up city traffic. A ladder attempt was made to rescue the pilot, since the cloud was low, but the would-be rescuer gained access to religion while halfway up, and nothing mortal was ever heard of him again. That's a well-populated cloud. But if it should rain, the inhabitants are in the Lord's hands.

Imagine how the passersby laughed. An orchestra of cackles, giggles, sidesplitting, and all other instruments of laughter, including a deep belly bass bassoon, was in full effect, until people's ears were dancing all over their faces. Corpses strewed the street, their intestines twisted into convolutions of laughter. It was a sheer hilarious occasion.

But my friend was deadpan, with a poker face so motionless that it would have been unmoved even by a calamitous explosion of incredible atomic strength performed just an inch and a half away in trembling meters of measurement, with the breath held and even explanation rationed brief. "You lack a sense of humor," I told him. "It's bankrupt," he said, in a dry feeble voice.

* * *

One day, as usual, I found myself smiling. It was futile to stop. Leaving the smile there, I looked for a reason. Not finding any, I opened my *Anthology of Jokes*, in order to justify my smile. I read a really funny piece of humor, worth almost a laugh. But when I consulted my face, I had only a blank look (according to at least one mirror, whose reputation of a fair verdict left no loophole for doubt). This was strange. I smiled falsely, but the affectation hurt my cheek muscles, so I knew that nature's heart wasn't in it. I began to fear an abnormal nervous system. Perhaps I would test my friend. He was handy. "Read this joke," and I opened to the page. As he read, his face flirted with an open smile, then warmly wooed her, and finally implanted marriage on the spot. His was the Adam and Eve of all smiles, exhibiting enough teeth to captivate a dental convention. The smile sagged in the middle, and rose hilariously at the corners, which fixed the expression for all time in its true classical archetype. Jesus having died on the cross for millions, my friend has just smiled for everyone. Today the world is hell. When my face is constipated for days, unable to soften the stonelike frown, I pray devotions to the memory of the smile founded by my friend, and if my piety is steadfast, I wind up saved. Faith alone is needed, if you'll forgive me for preaching.

* * *

Since my only fear is life, I go about dusting chips off my shoulder. Then I practice smiling in the mirror, to please my humorous friend. After playing back my laugh from the tape recorder, and adjusting the giggle when the static sounds mechanical, I'm prepared to endure his uppermost joke with the fortitude of a man. I keep my appointment only an hour late, and walk in with precise timing to the punch line. To do full credit to him, he does my laughing for me, to spare me from my worst fault: insincerity. After uncracking his several busted ribs, I lift him from his mess on the floor, and he vastly sighs like a furnace, to ward the hiccups away and keep his tears from splattering off the walls. "Was it that funny?" I ask, like a bewildered child. "It sure was," he whispers, barely audible; "next time you should have heard it. The style really tore my breath away." Then, with a heave, he replaces his wayward lung, and ventilates the used-up air. Then he smooths his blood down to normal, and tidies up his circulation, easing the wrinkles that time has placed in trust along the accumulated youth of his skin. Then he looks both ways out of one eye, to relieve his vision of surplus identity. He hairs out his comb, unwaxes himself of his ears, and nostril-pinches his devoid mucus. His manners were always on the safe side. He swallows a morsel of self-inflicted saliva, and sharpens his teeth with a slow grinding motion. Between his forefinger and thumb of one of his right hands, he lifts a word, capital letter and all, from the salty tip of his tongue. Having forgotten the period, he becomes verbose. Sidestepping an about-face, he trips in front of himself, leaving his past behind in a fruitless effort to catch up. Always modern, he lurches forward from one moment to the next. His memory is the neatest garbage collector on record. His life is conducted on a regular basis, leaving a day-by-day imprint of many of his most anonymous experiences. He is a self-enclosed history, an ever-moderning museum reinforced by an almost uncanny knack of poor taste. He does his eating himself, and lets critics do his reading. When he wants to relax, he soon falls asleep. His earliest form of exercise, of which he never tires, is an automatic yawn that keeps his jaws formed along an angular bone. He has a personal aptitude for food, and never falls in love unless he really feels romantic. When asked for his opinion on the latter subject, he remarked, "Love is only skin deep, and I'm not a surgeon." "Do you make love with dexterity?" I asked him. "No, I'm ambidextrous," he replied, while two of his sleepy eyes kept winking at each other. "Do they see eye to eye?" I asked, referring to them. "A couple of lovebirds," he opined, closing one and prying the other open with a toothpick he never tired of carrying. Then he scratched his nails with his loose remaining skin, and opened his closet to emit a noxious type of gas, at the conclusion of doing which, a semi-personal smile dominated the powers that mastered his face. "After evolution," I thought, "man comes next. The ill-fated example before me, with his fingers that always find themselves at the bottom of a bowl of soup, is one of nature's gentler masterpieces. He stands with one foot upright and the other in an open manhole, and is passionately interested in anything that confronts his attention. He must be a symbol. Lacking that, he is surely an end product." "Hear my joke?" he asked. "Why not?" I said, and already began laughing.

* * *

My friend is a composite, one half of him is a man. That's why he has such a strong sex urge. He's three-quarters human, which explains a whole lot. A goodly proportion of his makeup is given over to necessities, such as existing, to which he's bound by ties stronger than earth. At least thirteen/elevenths of him is fact alone, not to mention truth, to complete the picture. In addition, four/oneths of him consist solely of vice, frailty, folly, and, pardonably, vanity. One hundred/threes of this laboratory specimen is psycho-biological, with fragmentary evidence of socio-spirituality, due in part to the genes he inherited from God. Nor do these fractions tell the complete tale. Evolutionarily derived, my friend is a practical cabinet of chemicals, and what he does with blood, breath, and food is, if analyzed, phenomenal. But back to mathematics. Numerically speaking, my friend is, in large measure, quantitative, but even this must be strictly qualified. He drives God nuts. What is the ultimate explanation of his smile? There is none, but that doesn't stop him. Notice the curved line of teeth. The way the lips spread. The merry twisting of the eyes, giving out glints of light. And that breath-pimp, the nose, skin-folded where muscular contraction follows the due course, to insanity if necessary, of my friend's half-humorous emotion. Watch out. He's ready to speak.

* * *

My friend decided to be a king. "That's undemocratic," I said. But my friend looked in the want ads of an international placement employment paper, and saw an opening—a rare opportunity, especially for one of his humble birth. My friend put on a suit of his most refined manners, and applied as politely as possible. "The position is filled," said the interviewer, with an unmistakable foreign accent. "Already?" doubted my friend. "The ad is obsolete, it was left in from an old edition," explained that haughty bureaucratic clerk. "In fact," she added, "our nation is a republic now. The people rule. We have a job open as a farmer's apprentice. Are you interested? You would belong to the peasant class, with full voting privileges. In addition, there are bill-of-right benefits, and old age retirement pensions to go into effect the minute you die. The soil is fertile, you're guaranteed a crop and a wife. The rest is up to you, on a free enterprise basis, in case ambition is your obsession. No prejudice against immigrants—officially, that is." My friend stood up to his royal stature, and with a regal mien rejected the offer, bowed, and expressed his ingratitude. "How did you do?" I asked him later. "I was overqualified," he said.

* * *

"Does democracy include me?" asked my self-excluding friend. "Above all," I reassured him by exaggerating. "Then let me be king." "That's not equal." "Well I'll *make* it equal," he said: "a king can do *anything*." "But he can't vote," I said. "In that case," admitted my friend, "let me be a common man." "*How* common?" I asked. "Oh, common enough," he said, taking exact measure.

* * *

"I wonder what I'm really like," my friend pondered. I tried to be helpful: "What category do you fit?" "I'm not aristocratic or divine," my friend admitted, "so I suppose I come under the heading of common, as a regular practice. Does it bother you?" "No, I'm quite touched by it, in fact elated," I said: "you are, after all, on the sweet majority side, which ought to comfort your old age. (Myself, I'm superior, but don't mind me.) At any rate, I have a perfect description for you. You'll recognize yourself. It's an essay cataloguing common man, and in fact I had you in mind when I wrote it. My model!" and I smiled gratefully. "Well go ahead, I want to hear what I am, you're better than a mirror," my friend implored me. So I read from memory, with the help of the essay that I loudly read from, word by deliberate word, to help my friend know something about his own self-knowledge, from the toes of his top to the feet of his skull, not to dare leave out the crucial matter in between, or any extremity whatsoever, in his sociological anatomy under the species, "Common":

"The common man wields majestic power. He sees without eyes, and knows without learning. He marries with proud might, and sometimes pre-marries. His shoes are older than his feet, and his fingers always overrule the thumb's awkward veto. He need but speak, and language is immediately summoned. His voice booms thunder, while lightning flashes from his brilliant teeth. He votes. He goes to school. He works. He decides.

"His ancient foe is the world. Under a shady tree, he seeks protection, but rain runs him indoors. Once indoors, he opens his great library (a newspaper) and actually reads real words. His brain practically is self-electrocuted. He solves religion by saying yes, ignores war with no, untroubles himself, and sleeps inside a shell of the most selective dreamwork. He kisses his wife. He ruins her figure, and little children appear. He gives them names. And he is the center of attraction at his own funeral. But many years before he dies, he's sure to get drunk. His wild heart is full of instant biology. His laughter causes tears to grow. As natural as underarm hair, he acts his sincere role, moves contrary to his shadow, and disappears entirely. His old hag of a wife, a mourning apparition in black, sighs from her sour false teeth, and turns all her vacancy toward the stream of progress. The world is a shallow triumph. Its buildings are crammed with offices, and secretaries type a million words for every product that's bought or sold. The world is so old, it cooks up screwy games, and the people are being played. Common men are always born. There are so many of them, we have to smile in self-defense. We smile until our lips fall off, the stomach flops, the eyes search out blindness, and the dark feet reach, like roots, to the center of the earth. For every one who falls down, someone springs up. This army has great reserves.

"The collapsible sky, the Sistine Chapel of Creation, drives a shower of air into our daily lungs. I take a breath, and you take a breath. The common man is all nose, without fact. Should reality approach, he dives underwater and breathes through his trunks. His imagination is royal. It creates taste in his own image. In one Sunday, he undoes all of Creation. He wipes out nature, and streamlines progress, lifting his armchair to perch on the nearest convenient star. Though an absolute monarch, he keeps government under democratic control, and has spies spying on spies, to carefully check up on his own precaution. His right foot is constantly under vigilance from his left foot. He walks both ways at once, and sits down on opposite extremes. The closer he is to himself, the blunter becomes his sense of smell, and the duller his critical faculty. When he thinks a thought, the air stops breathing, and the sun is under eclipse. Once the thought is already thought, he gets up, and decides to act. He chooses or uses a wife, changes employment, melts crime from his hands with cheap soap, and buys a one-way ticket on the way back. He negligently leaves his footprints everywhere, for other fools to trip on behind him. Then he chides them."

"Except I'm not married, that's my portrait all right," my friend came clean, caught in the very act. He's common in the easiest way, simply by being. By passively not resisting, he makes it an art. "And don't dare be any different," I admonished him. "I'd never attempt anything so difficult," purred my contented friend. "Are you complacent, then?" I asked. "Without trying," he boasted, like a boy foolishly falling off his bicycle while pointing out, "Look, no hands," those two items referred to dangling in the waving air to join their owner on a downward cruise to disaster. "So far," he said, reviewing his life, "I'm precisely what I can't help but be." This statement impressed me, laden with ideal will.

* * *

The lecture ended which my friend and I attended. The scheduled speaker dealt with his subject. Now, in the general filing out, we too rose to go.

"Did you enjoy the lecture"? My friend asked me, while we were leaving the hall, caught in the crowded exiting of a profoundly subdued audience, with their sheep heads morosely looking down, shame torturing their privacy, and the act of being caught alive in the world proving, to each, a direct personal responsibility that never ceases to be both embarrassing and totally provocative of guilt. "Enjoy it? What lecture?" I answered in bewilderment, and threw all my resources into the pretense of having just awakened, and confessed that I had been sleeping the whole evening, from the first beginning word to the solemn last, and so absorbed the passed duration of that lecture into my blameless mind that was as freely guilty of innocence as it was deeply determined in the tradition of life-saving oblivion. "Was it any good?" I asked, and just then decided not to be born. The decision was a difficult one to make, but execution would be easy. And I should also avoid death, that other irksome responsibility. To my joy, then, I killed two poles with one interim stone, and live blessed with amusement that my crime not only goes undetected, but magnifies my happiness to an almost criminal grandeur, for I'm a martyr unmolested by torture, punishment, or by the damnation of recognition. I live lightly into a leaping grave, and then pay my respects to being born, without bothering to owe a moment's awareness to the grace or salvation of this tragedy we almost unconsciously breathe. Breath goes and comes, it is known, from and to a deeper, vaster, and more enduring source than this Johnny-come-lately, our little brittle Thought. Thought is like a nouveau riche, acting glamorous for the moment, clucking the extravagance of its foul pride; while breath always was, and never will cease to be, even if man himself goes broke, the animal kingdom ruined, and vegetables downtrodden with disgrace. Breath is a lasting effect, both before and after, but doesn't depend on such a flimsy foundation as life, no matter who or what does the coincidental living during the span of vacancy permitted to its unique organic structure. "The lecture was pretty good," said my friend, after giving the matter some thought. His breath knew otherwise, but remained a brilliant secret.

* * *

To my friend, day and night are all one. "Why discriminate?" he says like a Negro just before he's lynched. "Let's merge night and day," he advises, "to preserve the union. If Lincoln did it, why can't I?" So he sort of blends them together. The result is always twilight, but he calls it dawn, optimist that he is. When asked the time, he never hesitates to reply: "Dawn." He saves a lot of sleep that way. He saves so much sleep, that insomnia rewards his admirable freedom from segregation. He goes to bed with insomnia, and what with tossing, they produce bright mulatto children, and with turning those children are unborn again, while dawn mingles race and crime, space and time, the frozen hybrid too paralyzed to advance, and my stiff constant friend ponders the virtue of variety, to thaw his dilemma and send equality spinning onto the other side, where contrast waits to greet him. Then his talent for blending comes in, though he's so drastic, extremes are imminent, and polarities equally woo him, while he broodfully compromises his prejudices and softly flavors a liberal outlook, hiding archly behind his hypocrisy, and blackly fearing to call a spade a spade, and cringing whitely into a dream without color. Craving everything in immoderation, he betrays a downward tendency towards some neutral nothing. Then conflict dissolves, and a Negroid mask of harmony disguises mankind's variegated face of difference. And that's equal, with a black emphasis. Reversing the old supremacy, exchanging roles, and inviting a brown tyrant. Until the guilt is beaten down and atonement squeezes whiteness of all its sin and remorse. And the black man's boot pardons the white man's face. Or bootblacks it, for a nominal tip. With a shine, to see his guilty mirror. How the haughty shall stoop, and raise the low, until level measures a sameness without color, to celebrate a faceless democracy, clothing without skin, identity freed of ancestry, and brotherhood rages incessantly. And ferociously, with a brutal jungle twang, beast chewing up beast, stripping us of animals; until evolution undergoes a revolution, changes its policy, and makes our species constant, without change or variation. Then, we shall be equal. Equality shall be our dominant trait. If we survive, that is. What is fit? Selection. Selection how? Oh, by superiority, I guess. Who is? The human race. Except? Except some people, in spite of democracy. Then? Black equals white. To what extent? Both together, or the same. But what of differences? Illegal, and sharply outlawed. If you're different, you're jailed? Yes, but in segregated cells. Why? Oh, for old time's sake, that's why. But isn't that reactionary? We can't all be progressive.

When it comes to living, my friend insists on variety. First he lives on one side, and then on the other. In the end, he comes right side up, somewhat overbalanced toward the center, but flavored with a very liberal outlook. Anything he sees is always held at memory distance, full of the wisdom of perspective. He knows that prejudice distorts. So when he sees a black man walking down the street, casting a shadow equally black in the sun's indifferent democracy, my friend whitewashes his vision with kind tolerance and regards the passerby as an albino. The Negro is flattered, and stops to thank him. Their shadows intermingle, diffusing the brotherhood of man with a glowing blur, and furthering the definition of progress. My friend is taking lessons on how to become a Negro. This is a racial change of a serious nature, but the equality is ripe for it. It's got to be now. That means me too. I'm what my friend is. So black, here I come. As black as he? Aren't we contrasts? So, that's right. So I'll oppose. Let him be extreme, challenge the sun, argue with shadows, and I'll mock him, or point it out. Keeping on the safe side, to take the harm out of his own danger. Let him rave.

He's fanatically intent. When shadows are underdogs, he wrestles with the sun itself. On a very hot day, feeling humidly sadistic, I humored and provoked my friend's obsessed insanity and got him twisted about to whitewash the black shadow his backward body happened to be casting in the sun's tilting path. He's mad. He's color-blind in the elementary sense, and the horns of his bull's dilemma see red when caught between black and white. That's what society does, refining his instinct till instinct turns into a dirty rebel. His hallucination, however, is quite rational. Poor mess.

"The sun is unfair," I complained, mopping it off my brow, "because it never shines on shadows. Why discriminate against the dark? Equality is a place in the sun, regardless of position." "Or color," my friend added, and with an oversized broom began sweeping the remains of his shadow from under the rug of his feet, sweating for an honest day's labor. Turning around for a glance at his careless result, he detected from one of his eye corners that the same shadow was still there, although slightly tilted at some sharper angle. In a rage, he threw his broom away, but not before he plucked it down to the last straw, at which point it soon began to resemble a eunuch on a forty day fast. Then, bare handed, he assaulted his spinning shadow, somewhat in the manner of a snake with a stiff spine trying to swallow its tail. The struggling shadow put up a token resistance, like the mirror matching ugliness with the human image. Finally, their toe-to-toe combat began to lose hold, mainly because a cloud saw fit to wander under the sun. This left my friend in an out-sprawled position, yelling, "That dirty yellow coward." "So at last we have true democracy," I told him, while the first of several raindrops bounced indiscriminately off my head.

* * *

"Do you like Irish people?" I asked my friend, lowering my voice in case he happened to be Irish. He, not knowing whether I were Irish, and afraid to give offense equally to himself, since his own past identity was a washed-away pedigree or a concealed United Nations that tinted his lineage in a mystery color, closed up his answer in a vault of compromise, shrugged either of his two shoulders, vaguely asserted the use of his eyes, and concluded by performing a smile without any announced direction, using up half of his lower cheek in an effort to control it. "And do you?" floated up from the depths of his safety. Thinking on my feet, I fell down, where I delivered my thunderous "Just as you." This suspended our tolerance in a united front, kept men from falling under their equality, averted an otherwise unintended race riot, and kept all its stars stitched to the breeze-waving flag above the immigrant-melted frying pan of our broad land.

* * *

Feeling anti-logic one day, I went political-arguing. "Are you of the Republican faith?" I asked my friend in my usual firsthand manner, "or of the Democratic persuasion—which?" "I'm a day-to-day atheist," he retorted, "and twice on Sunday." "Then your vote is split?" "Yes, but one on more side than on the other." Gradually it was necessary to fight, each championing the other's right to a viewpoint. I hit him with a free-speech uppercut, while he hooked a liberty amendment to my jaw. Then, feigning democracy, I delivered a telling republic blow. Bleeding from the bill of rights, he drew me at inquarters, where we cast a stuffed ballot and went into a brotherhood clinch. The referee (God) fully segregated us, but in an offhand manner knocked me out. He counted the ten commandments, which I took lying down, a glassy stare flashing honorable defeat from my conservative and leftist eyes. Still dazed, I saw fifty stars, standing for my states of mind. Instead of twinkling, they blurred. This gave me a patriotic unity.

* * *

I played ball with my friend. He pitched. He batted. I watched. He won. That bolstered his ego. He got delusions of grandeur, like the mumps or chicken pox. It even affected his sanity, if any sanity remained after having been exposed to all the vicissitudes of his very uncertain life, fluctuating at a notorious level between up and down, with the up being always low and the down dropping out beneath him entirely. Such, in the long run, is life. If ever a guinea pig was human, the illustration lived to be my friend. There he goes. To a ball game. It might give him ideas.

They'll clash with other ideas, but what the hell? Nobody is ruined more than he already is. Suffering turns to joy.

Although unathletic, my friend went to a ball game. He enjoyed it nevertheless, and pretended he had played. "But your name isn't in the paper," I wisely informed him, glancing at the latest sporting results. "I went under a pseudonym," said that modest athlete, "in order not to be mobbed into counterfeit autographing by literally worshipping fans. Tomorrow I'll take my bat and hit the ball again for another home run. Then, to spread the laurels, I'll change my name to a new ballplayer and win an equal democracy for both sides." "You're on no team?" I asked. "I'm on every team," he said, and dominated the scene. I had to admire his courage. "But does the umpire upset you?" "Oh him?—he doesn't count." "Then what's the score?" "Why are you so result-thirsty?" he retorted; "just enjoy the game." "Do you pitch as well?" I happened to ask. "Only when I'm at bat," he replied. "Then are you a star?" "Can't you read a record book?" he said, and then we began to get literary. The conversation switched to libraries. "Any book you happen to take out, I'm the author," he tipped me off. So he was intellectual as well. Renowned equally for the bat and the pen. Forgivably, I was awed.

* * *

"Are you scared of the atom bomb?" I asked my friend. "I can always duck," he replied, swaying his head off his flexible neck in illustration.

We like to put all idle theory to the proof, so we waited for a factual plane to appear. Finally we saw one, miles high in a lazy blur off the top of the sky, but it went out of our vision without dropping an atom bomb. "We're at peace, that's why," said my friend, protecting his courage despite the serene safety that assailed us. True to summer, every tree was green.

A little boy kicked a large rubber ball. It was really a globe of the world. I could see the continents, painted orange against the blue surface of the ball. "Be careful of the world," I cautioned. My friend butted in. "The world can take care of itself," he boasted, stepping on the ball. It exploded. "That was my crystal ball," he said, and rushed to phone a reporter. The little boy bawled. "Don't worry, I'll get you another world," I promised. The park filled with a chorus of its green trees.

* * *

"Do you believe in war," I asked my friend. "Yes, but only for destructive purposes." "And in the validity of peace also?" I re-asked him. "Oh yes," he assured me; "peace has its uses, as well: during a peacetime emergency, hostility must be strictly rationed, and vast measures of friendly idleness imposed upon the public patience. It requires a Spartan regime of discipline." "War relaxes these tensions," I suggested. "Yes, war is a back-to-nature movement," he asserted, "an instinctive, almost Freudian, reaction against our synthetic peace treaties and artificial cease-fires." "Should peace be outlawed?" I wondered out loud. "Not permanently," he modified; "the human race needs an occasional uninterrupted weekend of self-repopulation, a legacy to future stockpiles yet uncreated. Moderation," he concluded, "is our wisest laissez faire restriction on war. After all, death can be carried too far. After that happens, it turns against us and destroys us all. Like fire and big business, it should be regulated within reason. Don't get me wrong," he added in defense of his savage virility; "As a self-sworn rearguard liberal, I'm devoted to the charming simplicities of war, its triumph of sheer outlet, in addition to the prudish refinements and feminine virtues that peace contributes to our well-rounded study of the total picture of Man."

"Then war is a man and peace is a woman?" I pondered, hoping to vary this life-and-death matter with some spice. "Yes, but the man is usually on top," my friend boasted, "and the woman can only respond with passive resistance." "Some women wage aggressive peace," I contradicted. "Yes, but that's a sin against nature," he replied, "and illustrates our degeneracy. I like my war and peace straight." "And you'll get it that way, too," I added, for the air whistled with diplomatic failure teasing the potent nuclear atom to cock its world-devouring phallus. A final orgasm threatened Creation.

* * *

"Have we any control over being born?" my friend asked in despair. "No, the job is done for us while we're sleeping, so to speak, and when we wake up everything is all set. We merely appear, like an ornate celebrity wheeled out in a wheelchair." "I don't remember," my friend claimed. "No need to," I said: "what need have us freeloaders for any special alertness? We're done for, and that's the whole job."

* * *

"Do you understand art?" I asked my friend. "Pictures? Not nowadays, no. But old pictures, yes." "Are you a moron?" I asked, tactfully. "Not always," he replied: "but art brings it out in me." "Perhaps if you understood artists better, you would tolerate their work." "All I know is that they don't conform," he remarked, and felt immediately complacent. "But please tell me all about them," he added, "because I'm determined to be polite, even if I have to listen." "I'll tell you about all different types," I promised, "and what their lives are like, and the subjects they paint." "Excellent, it'll save me a trip to the museum," said this Philistine gentleman. "But I can only describe artists, not their paintings, so go to the museum anyway," I insisted, hoping for his conversion. "When you get through," commented my friend, "I may never want to see a museum again, not even from the outside." "All right, then listen," I said, and recited these tales of moral horror and obscene scandal, a bourgeois appraisal of the unstable bohemian element:

"Artists are crazy. They must be. Logic knows no other reason.
    "An artist drew a model. She was a model who poses nude. Then when he finished drawing her, she changed into her mistress role. For that role she was only naked.
    "When the artist got through doing both, the woman had no clothes on. Only then did the artist tell her.

"A queer artist met another one. Panting with emotion, they painted the same picture. One did it from the front, the other from the back. The problem was how to hang it. They suspended it from the ceiling, halfway across the room. But one side had more light on it. This started an argument. They pulled hair out of each other's brushes. Then they threw paint. Some of the paint ran down the picture. It changed the meaning. So they stopped fighting, and thought of a new title.

"An artist stopped painting because he starved. They buried his unfinished painting. As for him, he was redone by a sculptor. Now he stands in a museum, and looks true to life. He has gained weight, too.

"Not all artists are men. One was a woman. She painted her own lips. When the painting was dry, she hung it out to be kissed. An art lover passed by. He praised her painting, but refused to kiss it, believing in art for art's sake. But she had to make a living. She became a commercial artist. Recently her lips were reproduced, in full color: Her daughter is a promising young artist.

"One artist did a famous painting. Just to make sure, though, he died. As expected, the price soared. But when it kept on soaring, the shock revived him: the figure was fantastic. But by reviving he cut his own throat: the price sank. He had to die again. But this time the public wasn't fooled. Eventually the painting was so unpopular, it could not pay for the second funeral: so the artist had to be burned.

"One artist was known for his private life. He guarded it so closely, that a national scandal emerged. To shy away from the publicity, he disguised himself as his own model, and lived in a secret compartment in his mirror. His paintings were so revealing, however, that the FBI easily found him.

"Take another artist: When he painted, the crowd never looked. Even on a hot beach in summer. Even on a jammed subway. He stood on his head. He painted upside down. But no one, not even a critic, took the time to look. Then he took his clothes off. He posed as his most intimate self. Again, the public had other business. Fanatic, he committed a hideous crime. At once, a policeman arrested him. He was tried, however, as a citizen. His artist status wasn't even noticed.

"One artist went on a sit-down strike. When he stood up, he was sitting on a pile of dung. To economize, he painted a picture with it. A critic, observing it stink, pointed out crudeness in the style. The public considered it bathroom art. That is where, even today, its many reproductions often hang.

"Another type of artist used a vastly opposite approach. He produced what, in his own phrase, were 'breath paintings.' He expelled his breath on an otherwise empty canvas. Like a flutist player, he varied his breath with great artistry. In his repertoire were included garlic effects, alcoholic renditions, asthma studies, halitosis abstractions, deliriums of bedroom panting, and sketches of the liberal air in various phases of rhythm. His art was criticized as being impermanent. Many of his past canvases, for example, seem faded. The truly old ones, it has been remarked, seem positively dated. Yet an approving critic, noted for his shrewdness, has labeled his art as highly vital. Said he (we quote), 'There is the breath of life in his art.' Recently, however, this artist developed an illness, and is presently recuperating in an oxygen tent. Should he die, which is likely, his style of art seems, to put it mildly, doomed.

"A woman was born abstract. To be cured, she was sent to pose for a realist. As more of her appeared on the canvas, less of her remained in life. As the painting took final shape, she narrowly disappeared. The artist, it had appeared, captured her totally.

"Another woman, feeling too important to be lost, posed for a full-length portrait. The artist, poorly paid, did nothing but buy a full-length mirror, framed suitably for the occasion. While posing, the woman prepared to be vain. The artist, concealed behind the mirror, pretended to not be idle. Then, to end their agony, he presented her with the mirror. The mirror stunned her, reflecting nothing but her surprise. 'How I move!' she gasped. 'Naturally, Madam,' answered the painter: 'Because my subject is vital.'

"Today, her portrait never stops exerting an immerse fascination upon her. The fatter she grows, the fatter is her realistic portrait. But she continues to be less and less flattered. The painter, meanwhile, is serving a libel sentence.

"One artist got stuck on the color red. The sea was red, the face was red, the tree was red. He toiled in the sun. The sun painted him red. In between strokes, between brush and canvas, between sun and him, his sanity developed a red clot, which spread, and drowned the reason in a sea of abnormal blood. So red was he, that a blush made him pale. Just at that moment, a leech appeared. As the blood drained and drained, and the sun ebbed, he lost all strength to paint, somewhat like a barbered Samson. His return to white sanity clashed with the violent appearance of night. He dribbled a feeble brush with colorless strokes upon a worn canvas, and roughly sketched a ghostly deathbed, his final act. Morning revealed the complete immersion of the artist with his work."

"Are those typical artists?" my friend asked. "Typical of some," I said. "But some weren't artists, they were only painted, why did you mention them?" "They throw light on the light that throws light on the painting artist." "You weren't always favorable, I thought you liked artists," my friend further challenged. "I paints what I see," says I, and won that little bout. "That last episode, why did you have to make it fatal?" he asked. "To be artistically proper," I replied, despairing of the futility. Was he really learning? "And why all the misery?" he asked; "And the pseudo non-reality? What moral can I draw?" "Draw a picture," I said, "and the moral is inferred." He stopped to think, which he's drawn out; he's still at his thought, years later.

* * *

Said my thirsty friend, "We can get intoxicated on modern art. And it will cost nothing, except visual insensitivity." "I can afford that price," I said, willing to risk taste for some shots of pure drink. Our eyes would be brutalized, but rise unsoberly to the head.

We went to an art gallery opening. It was free.

Feeling self-conscious, with terribly overinformal dressed people staring at us from under their cultural lids, we drank so self-defensively that we were soon as offensively drunk as they. Then, by resembling the crash guests, we were licensed to officially ignore the paintings that were crushed against the wall by an army of backs. This improved our aesthetics, between us, about two hundred percent, giving or taking a little in the marginway where minor errors violate the abstract purity of these statistics. The gallery owner asked us to buy. She was an it, I mean he was a she. Whoever it was, that ambiguous pronoun quoted so spaceship a price, my wallet crapped a leak through the zipper, heaping untold

embarrassment on what were, up to then, the manglebehaved proce-
dures of a socially artistic venture with ominous overtones of a definite
commercial character. The artist her- or himself, to our lucky embold-
ened surprise, became, after a manner, introduced. Critics and dilet-
tantes, the champions of fads, obscurity, and a mystical elite "Taste,"
flirted their wares unseen amidst the champagne subtlety by which the
evening had intrasophisticated itself. Presently, a painting came to view,
when a few people separated in front of a space of wall. This painting
was so abstract, the color curled itself away from nature and worshipped
its own remoteness. The "shapes" were so abstract that algebra had to
do double overtime since geometry fell sick at once. The "composition"
gave a design so irregular, a perspective so devoid of logic, a form-and-
space pattern so farstretchingly revolutionary in its extreme disregard
of even the loosest rules and thinly clad chaotic principles, that an
ancient veteran Academician resigned from his honorary Chairmanship
of the Board of Postmodern Art. This resignation automatically con-
ferred upon him the status of death, which he accepted in grim silence.
A makeshift doctor fabricated a heart disorder, so that the name of art
would not be smirched by a public scandal. A school grew up around the
artist. His imitators are so numerous, that for the sake of his reputation
he must copy them, since they are as far ahead of him as the future is
in advance of the past. I drank so much, that my friend fainted. This
made it easier for him to revive me, as the floor was tilting both ways in
a single stretch. The floor gave in, and became a mercurial sea. Fractures
of canvas floated at flood tide. A rainbow gave vent to an outburst of
full color, like a striptease dancer becoming suddenly nude. Each eye
fountained its own bath of sensation. How holy is our visual joy, if only
untainted by our tribal barbarism known as art.

We had an art hangover the next day. Our eyes felt like stomachs, and
our stomachs like eyes, trading functions and infirmities, going blind
and getting upset. The rest of us took sides in a balance of powerless-
ness, and deranged all projects, abandoned all acts, and stifled all duties,
making a strange harmony out of the unpromising elements of liquid
despair and constipated futility. "What do you make of art?" I asked my
friend, looking both ways into one answer. It was, "I don't know about

art. Will a museum teach me?" "It can try," I encouraged, and began to cry. The stomach cried, actually, because my eyes were busy belching, or bringing themselves up, or rumbling, or lunging upset or downset, churning the agonies of an organ at war with stable use and clarity. "I want to go to a museum," declared my friend: "Its safe old objects of old art ought to be a sodium bicarbonate against last evening's display of future newness prematurely unripe and nightmarishly premature. I want sanity and perspective at last. Classics and time-honored things are comfortably lodged in tradition, and can be properly appreciated by layman or connoisseur—or just plain art lover—during a bout of soberness. Their effects are not spiked, their highlights don't fizzle, but they're built into sturdy substance and conceived in the solidity of structure, whereby their merits endure soundly and serenely against the shifting webs of bedlam of today's marketplace art." "Then go to the museum," I said, "and tell me about it when you get back. I'm worse off than you from last evening, and mean to restore my culture on the commonplace level of sleeping." So my friend walked out, and I abandoned all effort to the heritage of the dream.

Next day I felt better. So obviously something was wrong. I was happy and lazy and tired. And ready to listen to my friend's interesting description of his memorable trip to the museum. We sat at leisure, or sprawled comfortably, and he said, "My verbal account will put you there as a spectator." "Very well, I shall be interested to go," I complied, and followed imaginatively his footstepping eyes through culture's wonder hall. He was a courteous reporter, and provided me with the welcome illusion that the self of my physical orbit was now contained within the finite universe of that wandering infinity, the vast museum. His words were gentle, resonant with the solid self-sounding virtues of placid culture and deep security in the everlasting.

"The museum is full of interesting things. All kinds of paintings are there. And then paintings too thick to put in a frame, that they call sculpture. And then there are spectators, with their scorecards, rooting for culture. And spectators of the spectators, looking for love's introduction. And art students taking notes. And old women trying to remember the past. And old men with too much to forget. And tourists, thinking that a museum represents a city. And loafers so poor, they study their soberness here.

"The museum puts staircases in between floors, mainly to unify the building. You grow tall as you go up. Meanwhile, fatigue smashes you down. When you leave the museum, your head is a corpse of dead paintings. You inhale vigor out of the air, and pray for nature to continue. You pause, and admire artistic leaves growing on a tree.

"While back up there, you were a mummy, with the pallor of ancient Egypt buried with you. You were Chinese porcelain, you were Greek bronze. You were ivory of India, and early American maple. You were dead things, gaudy displays of the permanent heart.

"The Negro in you wore those carvings. The martyr in you suffered the Crucifixion. The light that poured through those high windows did not come from the day itself, or through the city Chamber of Commerce. It came from the past, gathered on the drooping air, which weighed upon the museum and filtered through. Afterward, I took a bath. The more I scrubbed, the deeper was tradition absorbed, soaked through my universal body. When I took dinner that evening, the food shook hands with dead richness."

"Do you plan to return?" I heard myself saying, in response to his vivid description. "Yes, I returned while I was there, by going to the bathroom in between the various exhibits, and coming out again to resume my journey through those halls of a living past." "Other than the bathroom, was there any special side-adventure or extracurricular feature beyond the strict ken of your art study, worth relating for the fun of it?" I happened to accidentally mention, and was surprised by an affirmative response so enthusiastic that I wondered why he had omitted telling it on his own initiative, offering rather than replying. "Get set," he said, "for a mouthwatering exposition of the intimate relation between erotic art and simple untarnished eroticism. It'll make your fig leaf blush. It makes art worth living, and life one big work of art." "So you met a girl!" I forecast. "But 'how' is the trick, I stress the glamour and irony of my method, reducing the pickup technique to a formula of artistic example, abiding by the finest classic models, inspired by the hot central lust, stimulated by the unblushing vitality, of art in the raw, sophisticated infectiously and radiating its impulse of excitement to even the current beholder. Art buzzes with life, and the fallout reaches the timeless man and the timeless woman, teaching them to unite. Have I made you curious?" "So much so, begin at once." He smiled glitteringly, asserting the bold triumph of life-in-art, or at least, "how to live artfully." He looked like a pornographic picture cynically uncovered by the owner once the censor has passed out of the room, his investigation completed and the exhibition exonerated. Art is a vehicle for cheating, that life employs. Here's my friend's life-sized sketch of his little museum masterpiece:

"There in the enclosed museum, deeply down the Rubens room, I contemplated the Flemish nudes, who posed between lecheries for that flesh-ridden realist. And a contemporary living girl passed by, and paused. Right in front of a rape painting, featuring hooved satyrs molesting bulging white women, and from my view, the living girl fitted in perfectly with the perspective, except that unfortunately she wore clothes. Borrowing the imagination of a Rubens, I disrobed her, and her skin blushed a rich pink, in tint to the original stroke from the master's body-brush, wielded famously between his crafty legs, where inspiration flowed from and to his art, and the vitality was bruised with pleasure. Ah. But then the canvas moved, and my contemporary walked into another room, shaming the painting and paling its force. Loving art, I followed her. But no: she went into a polite Gainsborough room, full of propriety. Chaste, and no suggestion. Art with no blood. I waited. She moved. Down several galleries. Where were we? Ah! Here was Oriental abundance, the erotic religious sculpture of tenth-century India. No cold blue Gainsborough shadows, and the starchy overdress of respectable prudery: Here were the goddesses of fertility, eight-breasted monsters of beauty engaged in startling fornication—the sacred rites, the holiest of worldly obligations—with privileged princes, displaying postures of voluptuous temptation, suggestive of spiritual ecstasies. Where had my victim hidden? My contemporary equivalent? There she was, behind a large female carving in richly encrusted marble, whose eight or ten arms, opulently jewelled, all led and pointed to the ambitious space between the spread legs of that noble figure. It was my moment. I had hardly introduced myself, when a guard walked in. He saw that all was well, and left. I took the modern girl home, and made her my work of art. Oh lord, it was great!" and my friend crashed to the floor, grinning, like a thief who had eaten the impossible pie he had stolen before being unnecessarily captured by bored law officials. How jealous I felt! I waited for him to rise. It took all night. The moon was hot and gloomy, and sweated against my window. With dawn, my friend still had that grin, with his eyes wisely opened. "Life imitates art," moaned this sensualist, "and winds a vivid pulse around the figure of grace." I let this enigmatic statement go. His bliss was removed in purity from a world of casual non-art. A robust memory refined a taste no longer tame, but almost divinely wild.

* * *

"Do you believe in photography?" I asked my friend. "Yes, if it survives the darkroom," he answered, "and outlives its negative phase." I showed him a photograph of a pretty girl posing from the neck up in a bathing suit. He praised the interplay of light and dark, and liked the sexy way one of her ears stuck out from her combed hair. "But is it art?" I asked him, because I knew some photographers with berets who sold their pictures from art galleries. After he stopped laughing I turned an electric switch and shut off the sun, which is ultimately to blame for photography's rise as a fine art.

* * *

My friend listened to music. This reduced his hearing, like a retina exposed to too many firsthand observations of the sun, until memory alone was able to equip him with sound. "Comment tally vous," I shouted from the tip toe of my most sprightly lung, but his deafness by now had included French, so he answered in the universal language of a stupid frown, replete with a soundproof structure of silence which my human words were in no way able to penetrate. Inside, a phonograph needle was twirling a record of Bach. This I detected from the way he stamped his toes in counterpoint, going in and out in rotation like a bee among his favorite flowers. (Useless to add, his shoes were transparent, and his socks were knit together at odd intervals with holes.) But when

Bach had completed his abstract sermon, suddenly the noise of traffic regained its prominent perch on my friend's hearing. "How ugly," he proclaimed, "but I believe I hear your voice." It was true. My voice was beginning to assail him.

* * *

The phonograph jumped and pounced. "That's Bach," alerted my friend, so we sat at stiff attention straining our energy through our ears. First Bach was quiet, then he went fast. By the time we caught up, he dodged into something slow. We found the theme and retraced our steps, but then, in a dazzle of sound, the piece was over. "Got away again," commented my friend, as he turned the electricity off. "But not without a fight," I said, consoling us. To make room for the ensuing silence, I adjusted my hearing to the lowest normal pitch. This made it so easy to fall asleep, I did so without the slightest delay, putting my full heart in the act. When I saw Beethoven in person, it was so clear that I was dreaming that when I asked him, "Can you hear what you compose?" my wasted breath called me a fool, using loud sound language against its own master. Then, out of the clear blue air, like an ancient miracle turning new, the great majestic Beethoven actually answered me. Overjoy drowned my sense in a scream of deafness, but he spoke German anyway. "What did he say?" my friend was quick to ask when I woke up. "Nothing much," I casually offhanded him, and hummed a symphony. By Brahms, I think.

"But Brahms is too romantic," my friend insisted, with classical decorum. "*He* didn't think so," I replied, and finished the whole sympathy. Once the coda had sounded, bringing the monstrous affair to an end, my friend happened to mention Mozart: in what connection, I forgot. This was up my alley: I knew a thing or two I could say, he being one of our well-known composers, as well as famous, which is an expert combination for a dead Austrian to try to enjoy. "Do you know how Mozart was born?" I asked. "Yes, via his mother," my friend answered, forgetting music. This was an unforgivable lapse. "You don't know the *inside* story," I said, underlining "inside" with such undue emphasis that my friend detected a pun somewhere, or smelled it in the vicinity of the air. How right he was can be seen by the story I proceeded to tell, without skipping a note, and keeping sensitive key sharp in perfect pitch to the tone, sounding a hushed-up opus from musicality's muted archives in open censorship for posterity to hear:

"When Mozart had a pregnant mother (in those days he knew her from the inside), she had a fit of scare and went on to swallow a whole harpsichord. This gave him the advantage of early practice, before he made his official bow into life. With his midwife and mother for an audience, he played his own concerto in a brilliant debut."

"Well, he must have been a genius then," broke in my friend. "He still is." "But isn't he dead?" "No, but his immortality lives on." After a pause for reflection, he came back with, "But I thought *Bach* was a genius." "*Everybody* knows that," I sneered. "Yes, but they don't sound the same." Fiddling my fingers with impatience, I roared two perfect words at him: "So what!?" Cowed by two geniuses, he shrank into a minor music critic, who trembles at the slightest note. Today, his ears convert pindrops into major earthquakes. Put Mozart on the phonograph, and his air-conditioned sanity turns on its loophole and roars through Space. Or give one hint of Bach, whistled at odd hours miles from the nearest concert hall, and my friend joins his grave in one sweeping moment, where he tunes in short wave to the handicap forecasts of the Last Judgment, when early odds are placed on the most serious sporting event in the lifeline capacity of our human soul.

* * *

My friend is so crazy about music, and other cultures of aspect, he swoons in poise, and his sensitivity is alarming at so developing a rate, he almost ascends himself, and leaves the animal behind. Yet the animal does manage to prevail quite survivingly, as a fortifying base on which his pseudo-cultural superstructure is so elegantly poised, like a flea ballerina on the windy top of a coarse pyramid's monumentality. My friend has a way of surviving all disasters, inner and outer, with his mediocrity unimpaired and all his common resources intact. He's durable, stubborn. Clever, and cunning. A thorny problem pricking the greedy God of our doom. Is he immune to tragedy, and just to the side of our throbbing fatality? Being human is his only strength. Overdoing it, playing up to his strength, he grants himself a certain immortality. Which is foolish, since he always complains about life anyway. Being a contrary bastard, he prolongs things. He's a conservative rebel, and drives life simply simply insane. The sun is maddened, the moon is shocked. The stars hardly know what to do about it. They just sit there, and blaze. My friend does all the twinkling. If the world were to be crumbled up into one mold, the universe into one piece of clay, look, it has the form and figure of my friend.

Sensitive music, nature in a pose of culture, intellectually literary books, and enduring works of classical art are admired with universal passion by my highly developed friend. He has a refinement worthy of man's position among the superior animals. Even when he thinks subjectively, the thoughts are polished by sophistication. At home equally in a library or museum, and certainly no stranger to a concert hall, my friend is raised neatly above the fish and bird, whose instincts barely subscribe to more than the required subsistence for sea or air survival. What fish has heard of Bach, and what bird can do more than just pronounce Michelangelo? Shakespeare and the glories of sunset are also well known to my friend.

And yet, to balance out my friend's all-roundedness, it is fair to mention that he goes in for the wholesome pleasure that well becomes his virile manhood. To be both not a prude and yet genuinely cultured is, in our age of specialization, a mark of a rarely whole man, which I'm certain my friend is. He's humble, too.

But I just couldn't stand my friend. Oh, I hated him. I hate his perfections, which are so imperfect. I hate his way of seeing all sides at once, and so not seeing anything. His sensitivity is galling. I feel like ruining him. I want to utterly destroy him, as though he were a dirty piece of paper with my death warrant on it. There's something too precious, too wholesome, too enduring, and too brief, about the puny existence he makes of himself, exploiting space and time, duping art, making beauty a whore, and wearing out truth. God, I would love to clutch and belt him. All my pain would be forgiven, if just I might exhaust his feelings and so induce him to surrender the most excruciating pain from the bowels of his sense. This sounds so tempting, I declare, and the reward so brilliant, I'm about to tear into him and limb by limb reduce his formidable stature. What a holy joy.

My friend is awfully broadminded. When I hit him, he seemed to apologize. To make sure, I hit him again. He lost consciousness, like every inch of the gentleman he is. He breathes with cultural refinement. If a nose-blow comes on, he manages it internally, to avoid unfavorable or loud publicity. Elevating his voice to a whisper, he spills out a lot of memorized poetry, with the words gently rutted to their rhythm. "More, more, I can't stand it!" I cry. He wipes off my tears, and recites rhyme, like a parade of Nazis goosestepping past their Fuhrer. Drowned in sentiment, I muster a last "I give up," before a violent swoon annihilates my reason altogether.

His musical ear, I believe, practically composes the Bach or Mozart it symphonically hears. Every drop or drip of culture, be it an oil-color painting or a novel-type of story, is pre-chewed by my friend, and reduced to its most digestible cud. His purpose is to make art safe for democracy; as their broker, he manipulates art to shake hands with people, and glorifies the library, museum, and concert hall as appropriate places for common sense to keep out of the rain. His refined nervous system practically screams with delight when his eyes testify to a sunset. And the salt of philosophy tempers his art. When I choke him by the throat, for example, he keeps his dignity from salivating in poor taste. Tired of horseplay, I finish him up with a wallop. As his jaw rebounds from my friendly shock, I exclaim, "Wow, how sensitive he is!"

He never allows my brutality to interfere with our friendship, laughingly referring to it as "your little vice." This works on my funny bone, and while I writhe on the floor, with knees doubled up like an epileptic, he serenely smiles at the effect, like a sculptor looking at his statue from a distance in the park.

One year, when spring came, he led me from the house in order to impress me with the beauty of nature. "Just look at that tree!" he shouted, smitten. The sight was too much. "How could leaves be more sweetly green!" I managed, just as the nearby perfume of lilacs swept my senses into an ecstasy of pallor. As I was tilting into a coma, my friend threw up his arms and sang for all the skies to hear, "America, I love thee." Suddenly I became patriotic. It was too peaceful to join the army, so I offered a prayer to God, who put spring in America. Then I offered my friend, as a sacrifice. He knelt, and said, "goodbye." "Goodbye," I answered, driving back the tears with my clumsy fists. In the process, I damaged his eyes. Partially blind, he sails into the land of bliss. When the garbage collector sweeps him up, I hope for an anxious peace to settle among his driven bones.

* * *

My friend decided to become an artist. He painted. It turned out lousy. Then he took up poetry. But it couldn't rhyme. So he wrote a novel. But it had no plot. Then a play. But it was unactable. He tried everything. He danced, like a primitive. Like an ancient. Like a modern. But there was no coordination. The legs fell out one way, and the arms turned about this way; while the torso didn't know which to follow. But then, like a stroke of genius, he became a composer. But, being tone-deaf, he was also unmusical: No sense of rhythm, and he even screwed up a beat. So he made sculpture, in wood, stone, everything. No shape, it remained flat. And the relief was too round. He built a house, but it fell down; so he gave up being an architect. He acted, and played every musical instrument, but simply had no skill as an interpreter. In any field. It was disgraceful, not being an artist. Yet he had the soul of one.

Then he turned critic, and criticized all art, and got really good at it, so good that he outlawed art. Now anyone caught being an artist, or even pretending to be one, is strictly on the down-and-down, he's a no-good cuss. My friend saw to this. People are protected. Art won't harm them. My friend is a shield. And any former artist isn't allowed to reproduce. This is a great boost to science. Think of all the changed careers now.

* * *

"I like everything to be appropriate," my friend specified, like a woman examining bargains through a window and deciding not to buy because the store is closed due to its being Sunday. "You're fussy," I reproved him. "It's only my due," he stated, like a pay clerk slipping himself his weekly salary check when otherwise occupied by looking the wrong way, out of the window generally, or at least up to the clock, where the slowest pair of hands in the world are moving backwards towards Monday and depriving him of an expected weekend, it being probably Friday, and his boss up to his neck in a lot of troublesome profit, and the secretary involved in being such a sexy woman, which is what she was before she ever got hired in the first place, and despite such external things like a typewriter, which she finger-presses while keeping her breast locked up in that private cage, herself.

"I've got taste," my friend declared, "and plenty of it. I use it against art, against nature, against anything. I use it up all day long, and I still have enough left to keep myself going the next day, but a cup of coffee helps too, and a pill or two." "What's your goal?" it occurred to me to ask. "Getting somewhere, that's where," he replied, and intensified his ambition.

* * *

"Aren't you employed?" I asked my friend. "Well, no: You may say that I'm self-unemployed," he answered, pumping some life into his sagging pride. "Oh," I said, impressed: "then maybe you can lend me some money?" "Sorry. It all goes back into business." "Every penny?" "Every penny." "Well tell me from start to finish: Just what has been the work cycle, the success progress, of your up-to-date life beginning in the past. You may inspire me."

"Without trying too hard, I succeeded, but in the wrong thing.

"So I tried all over again. Gradually, I undid it.

"This restored my confidence. So I stopped doing anything.

"Gradually, the reputation of a loafer applied to me. This was my profession.

"I joined the union, but the dues were too expensive. Indignant, I became a capitalist.

"That's where all my money goes, nowadays."

"Well, I'm not inspired," I admitted, but was guilty of following his example before I had even known that there was a model for my idle industry. "All play and no work," I said, "makes loafers shirk." My friend approved of the rhyme, but was conservatively puzzled, or ponderously reactionary, as to the moral implied, or otherwise intended. But thinking was not paid for, so he soon stopped that foolishness. Myself, I was very pleased to think, because my business is strictly nonprofit. For tax reasons.

* * *

"Do you work for a living?" I asked my friend. It was a practical question. "I work, but not for a living," he reminded me. "What for then?" I asked, more practical than ever. "To earn a few bare essentials from money." "That's not living?" I requested. "No, it's only surviving," he estimated, like an auctioneer appraising the value of a doubtful antique before a few bidders whose only solid profession is that of begging. "What do you call living, then?" I asked, full of economic curiosity. "Not having to work," was the reply. Stunned, I allowed our silence to erase the dialogue in the blue funk and fog of drifting time. "Time for me to go to work," I said, taking my friend's monumental example. My pockets were empty, and my pants were even empty of the pockets, and my modesty and shame was almost devoid of the pants. He advised me not to bother. Then I must vehemently insist. Weakly would I oppose him. "I guess I should go out and get a job," I said. "No hurry," said my friend, while nonchalance collected about him, like flies around spoiled meat. "I agree with you," I said. Hourly, we were growing poorer. And that was at least progress, and gave us something to do, as well as described what to be. We had embarked on a momentous decision, as the stern consequences would soon so decisively indicate. Brute poverty was Reality's snarling answer, to our improvident defiance of its steeply practical authoritarianism. Could souls poetically meek be a barricade against the totalitarianism of a world indicting disarmed pennilessness? And had we courage or laziness to thank?

* * *

Here's a compound entry by my poor friend in his misery-tear-swept journal of a week or ten days of his poignant, methodical debauchery of his doomed life's time in his poetically heroic struggle to fill his soul with a sufficiency of body. (Speaking of body, all footnotes for this entry have been editorially omitted, to preserve a fidelity to the body and keep its text-appeal intact.)

"Being in between traumas, I looked for a job that wasn't hard to do. Finding one, though, was difficult. As I was about to succeed in failing, I found one. The blow nearly retarded my development. But with my first week's pay check, I found the incentive to survive.

"Friday at five o'clock, set at liberty, I walked to the nearest subway. As usual, it was the wrong one. Having paid the maximum fare, I was determined to look stubborn. But when the express came, I was a push-over. I took it to the first convenient station.

"The crowd proved my undoing. For a while, I was a mass animal. I even grunted like one.

"By then, the momentum was too strong. What fun it was to not resist! I tried harder and harder to not resist, until my soul shook hands with my body, and a horselaugh spread out between them.

"The view enlarged, and gradually, as my senses swooned, my ear played independent drum to a musical piece.

"Dividing, the crowd left me in my hole. Climbing out, I fell deeper in.

"Since spring returned to normal, I traced rhythms in the buds, until I met the flowers themselves. What smells!

"This led me to follow my nose. But the wind vanished, leaving hardly a scent.

"Monday, I returned to work. But it wasn't there.

"Regretfully, I quit. The subway waited earlier than usual. I made a natural mistake, and had plenty of time to erase it.

"Behind the buildings, April, May, and June, without hurrying, turned the slow pages to my life."

However my friend did, I fared equally worse, greedy for adverse competition.

When my despair was lowest, I discovered my friend shaving (indoors, if possible). "Why are you doing that?" I asked him, glad to have found him, and glad to share whatever pain I could spare with my tried and true buddy, my ego's altar, generous recipient and foremost scapegoat of the worst my life had to offer. His visage delighted me. I accepted him, I could eat him up. But this shaving business puzzled me, so assiduous was its frothy application, for he shaved on both sides of his face at one time, using two razors in the process, and employing both hands. His dependence was so acute, it even necessitated a mirror, as he was glancing back and forth at his own image, using both eyes while so doing. What a marvel of technique. He did enough shaving to take care of five beards, and sold a pound of his flesh to some exacting Shylock of vengeance. The transaction was with blood, for change. My friend never overlooks a secret. "I'm shaving you as well," he explained. I placed my hand over my cheek. It was true. "And for future occasions," he inserted, to account for the multiple quantity at one fell slice. I bled in several places, to exceed his finely spouting fountain. "Does it hurt?" he asked. Where did our pain emanate from? His jaw almost perished, as his transferred nerves were recorded at a delicate point in my chin's jolted terminal. Was sadism the link most mainly connective between the disjointed particles of our very fractured friendship? Was not enmity bred by our familiar transgressions of privacy's sacred boundaries, which we violated as an intimate rule? There was a desperate flaw in our relationship. To mend it was not difficult merely, but by now desolately undesirable. What greater hopelessness could we ask for?

* * *

Employed in a drab office, my friend worked hard to wait for his natural coffee break. But his tediously clerical duty was relieved, with the arrival of that refreshing minute. He walked off, anticipating his revival.

He took a long coffee break, from which he never returned. The firm mailed him his back salary, up to but not including that coffee break. This enraged him, so that he quit. Now he is a freelance coffee breaker. Companies hire him to go back to work in time, setting an example for the other employees. Then, when they have followed him, and are established at their desks, his job is over. His professional title is "morale expert." His fees are small, but the coffee is free.

* * *

My friend read a science book. It was phenomenal for facts. My friend took it matter-of-factly, which pleased him so well that he converted to materialism, a solid religion which he practices daily. It has rewarded him with money, as a practical answer to all the worldly prayers he says in a frenzy of ambition. Now a fanatic, my friend treats facts like God, and wears a halo of realism, and his diligence is paying off, he's a typical modern business angel with his feet squarely on the clouds. Yes, he's going places, and has a divine income. He'll marry God's daughter, and take everything he has with him, above the top floor, with a nice air-conditioned tomb as a living monument to the hard-earned success, the honest cash he has sweated to make. My friend is a self-made man. The rewards keep pouring in, concrete as hell. He roars at top efficiency, the sky's the limit, and nothing's so sure as the tax of death. His capital investment sings a profit hymn, watch him go.

"You have lots of money now, don't you?" I asked jealously. "Try to get some," he challenged, and viciously proclaimed himself a miser with his newfound wealth. "Why? Aren't I your equal?" I asked, begging. He scornfully laughed. "In soul maybe, but not in good old money," he said, and counted his banks, charging slight interest on himself to make the investment worthwhile. What a practical schemer. "Please explain why you're cruel," I asked, and invoked our friendship. He said that friendship had nothing to do with it. Money was money, and that was that. A purely impersonal gain. Bound by its own rules. Multiplied by its own selfishness. Exceeded by its own gain. And protected by the wise caution of the born miser. He proceeded further:

"I do have, at heart, the soul of a miser. Money is worth money, and is loaded with relatively dear value. That's why I save it. When I spend, you may be sure it's to buy something, otherwise my waste is heedlessly extravagant and amounts to a loss which, in effect, reduces gain, when one accounts for it. Be dolorous, if you have sense. Nickle down to a thrift in dime save penny quarterly if credited with interest, you can bank on it. Money is like love: one thing not only leads to, but is followed by, another. Then when too much comes, it's an additional bonus, sweet and tidy. Ah, life. It's great."

He smiled a genuine smile, and felt in a good mood. Security had eased his pain. He no longer had to drink coffee for a living. His wish had come true. He was rich, famous, and miserly. He could lecture all about money, and had it to count. I had much to learn from him. Envy was a great teacher. But was it natural we should be so uneven; he so more, and I so less? Or would heaven make up the difference? And would I get a square meal there? Or was eating impossible, because the stomach just didn't care? But here below, money starved me because I didn't have it. Would I pay my teeth for the pleasure of eating? Or just for the thrill of holding a unique dollar bill? My pride was cast away, and I was wanting. I was subject to the worst deal. Eminently exploitable, and without power to resist. Which is justice, almost defined. And while I'd pout, my friend would lavish a laugh. And be large, grand: superior, and dignified as he was rich. And so the world protects its proportion. Conservatively, the scale is kept. The humble remain, and the privileged can expand and gloat, because the currency they possess has transferable honor and everywhere reflects on the owner's unimpeachable prestige, and thorough dignity. How servile I must fawn. And cow. And be a dog. And withhold my bark. And beg for the least bone. And what will he throw me? My own. Or I must donate my tooth, for a slighting interview. How ignoble I'm held. Or is my friend bluffing? Let's see the proof.

"Money is natural, being the same more or less color than glass—I mean grass." My friend told me that while counting the contents of his wallet.

"Then I'm not natural, because all I have is silver metal," I told him, and proceeded to jingle my more or less otherwise empty pockets. The music suffered from a hoarse throat.

"Are you allergic to green bills?" my friend gently asked. He held one out, after dusting it with a pocket-sized whisk broom.

"How I envy its inherent value," I observed, and calmly studied its clean and well-identified regularity.

George Washington grinned at me. Fools will tell me he is dead, but one's portrait on an American dollar assures one's immortality of a stupendous reign of longevity.

I took the "paper" from my friend—borrowed is the word—and held it, lofty with translucence, in the path of the sun. Peering through with world-blurred eyes, I saw a mirror of my poverty: penny eyes, nickel nose, quarter ears, and dime teeth. "How worse than a skull," I raged, "to see a live face—one's own, too—flashing the cheap metals of its own disgrace."

Replacing the dollar into the careful possession of my friend, I dislodged a loose tooth in payment of tip, acknowledging my debt to wealth.

My friend put George Washington into his spending pocket, and found an empty place concealed among his smiles where my ex tooth was given a new livelihood. It did not flinch under the pressure of steak, despite the novelty of the experience.

I, meanwhile, chewed some juicy germs that had gathered in the waning air. Saliva made an excellent dessert, and served for toothpaste as well.

* * *

My materialism is limited to money. Paper money is lighter than metal money, but more expensive. Money tests friendship. I asked my friend for a loan. "From me to you," he answered, "no; from you to me, yes." I admired his honesty. "Well, you're a good businessman," I reluctantly admitted, and gave him the amount I had wanted to borrow. Faced with hardship, I had to do without. I swallowed air for my breakfast, and washed it down with some new saliva I had secreted for the occasion. Then I brushed my teeth with a frenzy of vigor, to keep up appearances. I stuffed a pillow under my belt, to let the world see me as myself. "Pride is my only liability," I often confessed. I walked out into the street, flaunting a vulgar toothpick. "How disgusting," people whispered. To further convince them, I doubled over and made as if to vomit. It was all dry and imaginary. While all this was happening, I was secretly losing weight.

Sympathizing with my plight, gravity released her hold on me; immediately, I felt much lighter. I practically floated along now. "He's putting on airs," people were saying. "His head is in the clouds," some practical people asserted.

Squinting hard, my friend almost saw me. The weather was good, and I have a sharp profile. Otherwise, space had almost hidden me. "Do you want your money back?" he asked. After darting back and forth along the sliced air, the sound waves conveyed the question to the tin buttercups that were once my ears. After swallowing, I was able to talk: "If you can afford it—" "No I can't," he gleefully replied, and bulked his wallet back into his pants.

Then I got into the garbage can habit. The cats bitterly fought back, but I got my daily scrap. Health assaulted my cheeks, turned the blood current on, fed thought pap to my starved baby brain. From all directions, muscles converged on me, some fitting and some unfit, while my distressed skeleton hid somewhere in the middle. The sin of vigor glowed in my loins, and my internal system was a living chemistry where juices, hormones, and pep discharged atomic energy from simple human elements. "How handsome,' screeched the women. "Here's your money," timidly offered my friend.

I carefully counted it, and found a penny missing. "Service charge," he simply remarked. It forced me to cough. Then I discovered I had a cold. From starvation? No. My friend's germs were on the returned money. That's what he does. When he takes, I suffer. But let him once give, and I've had it. Even if owed, a debt discharged by that unwholesome creature boomerangs to obligate the creditor in the fiercer violence of some new misery, all is loathsome that he touches. "Please keep it," I said, and referred to my penny. Too late. He had spent it.

* * *

My friend was out of money. He applied to the bank. "Do we have your name on file?" a teller asked him. "No," my friend truthfully replied.

"Then go away, especially if you're a bank robber," he was told. My friend wished he had money. The wish became wealthy, but my friend remained poor.

"Have you money to share with me?" he had the nerve to ask me. "No, I have only private money, and it's not transferable," I said. "But I have a real need," he reminded me; "desperate, urgent." I gave him all the sympathy I had on hand, and the promise of more should it ever run out. This rekindled his faith in human nature. His heart warmed over twice, frying itself sentimental. He shook my hand, and the sparks very nearly burned me. "I would kiss you," he said, "but you're not a woman." Blushingly, I agreed.

Next time I saw him, he looked hungry. "Man can't live on sentiment alone," I remarked, with my well-fed cheerfulness. "No," he said, overhearing me. The "no" had no weight behind it. It came out of a hollow container, part of a general overall emptiness to which his physical plight had reduced him. "I'm in reduced circumstances, as you can tell," he described himself. I decided to flatter him: "How true!"

Next time, he announced his death. "So soon?" I gasped—"not already?" His skull smiled, ironic, but gentle. "That's unforgivable," I said, morally outraged: "Can I advance you a dollar?" "No," he sadly declined: "I'm not supposed to take it with me." "Go on," I implored; "no one will know." So he stuck it between his ribs, and right away it began to earn interest. "I'm leaving on a sour commercial note," he announced, hiding his soul in shame. "Get on with you," I prodded, giving him a good-natured dig. "Yipe!" he yelled, from the poke in the ribs. Deftly, I had removed the dollar, and left him the interest, with all my good wishes. He died poor, vowing to come back. "With what?" I shouted after him. He couldn't even pay for his passport. Space took all his remains. The customs officials confiscated his poverty, and now he's a free-loader, living off the fat of the land, floating, a drifter, an entertainment figure who's looking for an angel to back him. "Your head is in the clouds, you dreamer," I yelled up. He ignored that taunt, snubbed his non-nose, and enjoyed the extreme luxury of death, like a king but belatedly crowned.

* * *

My friend let loose, and sneezed. The air carefully gathered itself together again, after being locally at odds with prevailing climate and momentarily boycotting the trade winds. The germs were assimilated, like immigrant Jews within the overall commercial prosperity of uniform America. My friend, who had recoiled, was now well distributed in equal blocks of masses behind the reformed nose, whose recent adventure was put aside with even temper as but the sowing of wild oats. The nose, to compensate for its rash act, became a model of decorum, and was elevated as a moral precept: seen, but not heard.

My friend put his eyes plainly out of sight, adjusted his many thousand hairs along the wavy teeth of his comb, and spent his posture bent just upright, defined by a curve on which hung the dignified bearing of his kind, the species of advanced standing in which he ranks as a lifetime member.

To be sure, however, he consulted a mirror. "How true to life," he remarked, appraising it as a work of art. The tired mirror, bored with endlessly duplicating him, sighed for its thankless toil, turning out thousands of images a week to provide my friend's vanity with the qualms of doubt and the illusions of reassurance. And all my friend ever paid the mirror for its efforts, was attention, which by itself was hardly worth the cost of a new secondhand pair of shoes, at the current demotion of the God-forsaken dollar, the weightless pound, and the air-filled franc. Not to mention the extinct mark. But these are worldly matters. Trifles, merely. Starvation is their only consequence.

Speaking of which, my friend sat down to eat. His intake was considerable, and the food never had a fighting chance, but with passive resistance went down the ravenous pit of destruction. Celebrating this uneven slaughter with a moderately alcoholed drink, my friend praised his inner standard of living, giving premium gratification to instinct's nature-working glories, serving vital delight to that sense-intoxicated organism—the Lord Body itself—with which my friend was flattered to be associated, and whose connection he was at pains to maintain, even at the expense of having eternity's benefits curtailed momentarily and appeased with the frantic courtesy of delay. "It was a good dinner," said my friend, and the remark was gradually overheard by himself. He was good at these echoes, passing meaning from his brain to his ear while saving himself the expense of unnecessary sound. He was frugal, and could have enjoyed a splendid career as a miser, for which nature talented him, if only he didn't lack one thing: money. Were it not for that deficiency, he would have been arrested as a monopolist, an old-fashioned slave trade capitalist whose vast accumulation of wealth summed the entire treasure of the universe, amounting to quite a pile of riches, and a sizable bank account as well, in addition to loads of money, as an extra dividend. As it turned out, he was poor.

So he went over to me and asked for a loan. There never was a franker smile on anybody's face than the one that lit up on mine when those incredible words were admitted to the stingy courtyard of my hearing. The description of the smile, boring my reader, would consume thousands of my publisher's pages for each volume of this worthy book, and be of interest only to a dentist maybe, whose sharp commercial eye would spot scores of cavities and conclude neglect at the gruesome spectacle of decay, since my mouth is a hideous cemetery where premature death has a field day, a picnic for hosts of ghosts dangling nerves, like wires from fallen telephone poles, that still ignite with the liveliest sensation of which man is capable, the pang of pain.

"No, I can't lend you anything," I said. This upset my friend. "It's only money," he argued; "I don't want your hand or your foot." By itself, the conversation was led to "possession," and its legal, moral, psychological, phenomenological, actual, apparent, supernatural, and Godly aspects. We had to conclude, the two of us, that what we owned totaled nothing, give or take a quantity here or there, to balance an even roundness of figure, as a formal recognition of hypothesis, to blot out realism's pain with elegant mathematical abstraction. "Intellectually this is very satisfying," my friend said, "but bankbook- and wallet-wise, this practically comes down to nothing." "It's a gift then, not a loan," I said, with a generosity I barely managed to afford.

Dignity remained to my friend. Having sneezed his nose and eaten his meal, the kingdom of himself retained access to dignity, beyond which, and lacking it, loomed a tempting void that would swallow his discouraged humanity and divorce his existence from what, in confidence and faith, he proudly called his soul. There was much to buy, and much to be unbought.

* * *

As for a description of my friend, his height has always been approximate—even more so now that it has stopped fluctuating. Remember that when he sits down, his height has a tendency to fold up. His weight is supported by gravity, and until it stands on its own merit it would be a scientific understatement to burden fact with figure. For his skin coloring, the rainbow has nothing to fear by way of rivalry. His hair is well placed. His laughter is a combination of open smile with sound effect. It is rarely ever contagious. Neither his thoughts nor his soul are visible, and must be assumed. His identity is no secret, but anthropologists haven't given up yet. His name describes him only superficially, and is somewhat dated by now. By repeating a given act, he is soon converted to habit. Yet the weather is far more predictable.

His behavior blends virtue with vice, and yet betrays neither. Morality could hardly survive on his example alone. His private life is open and his public life is closed, while he lives somewhere between, not so much lost as simply not found. He obeys all the rules of psychology in both act and feeling, since he knows how useless it is to refute science. He comes from natural ancestors, and now only nature remains.

Death in no way scares him, unless applied to himself. He practices survival daily, until it flows regularly through his circulation. To be official, he prays. In the politics of religion, he stands forth unanimously on a God ballot. As Vice Deity, he sweeps himself into power, which he mismanages grossly. Slightly to the left of human, he indulges chaos until all principles collapse. After that, he polishes up. Collects the spoils. Re-elects himself. And sits back, smug. You can just see the lack of cigar, and smell it, in his grim mouth. Altogether, a character example, of the type to be avoided. Evil, beautiful: because pure. Good, therefore.

Which can be argued. Here's where judgment comes in. Unbiased, like mine. With no ax to grind, except on my friend's head. Which, nevertheless, still stays on. But the ax falls off. We bury it, permanently. But buy a new one immediately. Defense, you know.

Is my friend good or bad? Are there any attenuating circumstances? Or is he both good and bad, and so destroys morality altogether? Is he symbolic? Or if not, can he still manage to be real and illustrate only those virtues and vices constitutional to his own individual necessities, and so spare the world the trouble of bothering to emulate him? Where is he, in the scale of things? And why there, of all places? These questions may commend him, but the answers are not for sale, cheaply frozen in the unknown. Conjecture and prejudice pluck at this forbidden knowledge, and appetite whets the desire. How should I regard him?

My friend is kindness, personified. He never practices it. It never once enters his behavior, or even influences him, but nevertheless, my friend is kindness itself—but in reverse!

Oh, he's foul. And foul is no word for it, not a word is alive that can describe it. What is evil? Evil can only be defined by my friend, and derives its particular connotation from every deed, misdeed, or anything else for which my friend is directly responsible, judging by his behavior. And yet, he's not such a bad guy.

I estimate him subjectively, that's true. It helps to balance out my emotions, and actually to objectify some semblance of order once I've been through the mill of my private ordeals and have been exposed to life through the directly personal route at the tip-ends of those naked nerves that risk the mental torture of pain and gamble for the rarity of pleasure. As a frequent loser, I have my friend to fall back on, to take the heat, and wear the edge, off the daily suffering wounds I lick after the contest of deadly give and deadly take that mark my disastrous play in the loaded game against me. "No dice," says the fatal arbiter. Then I settle on my friend, and we exchange the trivia of decorative smiles, to foolishly purge ourselves of the unseen tragedy reigning overhead, to which in breath and deed our foremost souls are bound and despairing hearts must earnestly repair.

After events have settled themselves, I'm left holding the booby prize of my emotions. My emotions are internally confused, since they deliberately rebel against the orderly world of fact. My emotions are governed by a sense of anarchy, and are disciplined by the laws of chaos alone, which throw a romantic coloration all over the inward feelings which are so subjectively personal to my life. However, I have a friend. He can be identified as not-me, so he helps to balance my perspective. When I recognize him, a certain sanity comes over me, I can't explain it. This sanity is a double-thick mystery, under the protective coating of our combined insistent ignorance and graceful curiosity-resisting stupidity, until the mystery takes on the semblance of truth, the assurance of dogma. Yet, still we're uncertain.

* * *

This one particular day, as I recall, there I was, having an emotion. Compared with my friend, that wasn't much, because he was undergoing an emotion. After he stopped, I tried to soothe him. I opened the window, and force-fed him some of the latest air, hoping that it was still hygienic to breathe. (Fashions change.) "Any traces of that emotion?" I asked, when he seemed calmer. But my strategy backfired, because the very *mention* of emotion gave him both a setback and a relapse, which not only damaged his recovery, but was emotionally upsetting as well, and made him undergo another emotion so strong, bones and muscles all over his body began to go on strike, demanding more pleasant working conditions and more frequent coffee breaks, as well as a production rhythm that had less stress and calmer interludes. A vast reduction of overtime was also demanded. "Thank God my troubles are only internal," said my friend with an evident sigh of relief. But by coincidence, an atom bomb fell that very moment. It landed only a block away, so we had to run fast. "This is a great cure for hiccups and emotions," said my friend, joining in the panic.

With a wartime emergency declared, and an overall disaster acknowledged, the bones and muscles inside my friend had to stop striking, and the differences were settled by peaceful means, like compromise and other humanely Christian inventions. It was quite a long span of time, then, before my friend regained his capacity to suffer with emotion. The business at hand crippled one's privately domestic preoccupations, and emotions had to be outlawed in the strict face of an explosive world.

Once the atomic hellocast had subsided and a generation of entirely new survivors had repopulated the sagging population with a throbbing and

109

indeed seedy excess of derived and imitative vitality, my friend crept out of his shell, or emerged confidently from the cave, as a fragment of his former self, having hibernated prehistorically in the dawn of civilization's belated dusk, and was now a retarded product of an emergency metamorphosis, with his body intact but with his soul splotched with history and simply riddled all over with the allied impact of disastrous experiences and earthshaking events. "Whew, what a close call," he said. My hearing was impaired by the latest catastrophe, but I pretended to understand. Once more, it was safe. We could walk the streets. Breathing went free, with occasional asthma intervening. Our faculties slowly awakened, and seeing was done through the courtesy of the eyes. Normality approached us, but being a snob, we ignored it. Even, finally, we had recourse to laughter. It was a refuge, and we spent it in extravagant volleys, tearing gaping alleyways in our lunging sides, through which agony could emit air. We were undone, all over.

With the air cleared, so to speak, my friend was once again encumbered with the irritant of emotions, dividing an uneasy soul from a body-tormented mind, and he lapsed into a grave mood. It looked bad. I'd doctor it, and patch him up.

My friend was in a mood. When he recovered, he landed in the opposite mood. Jolted by the transition, he became moody. "Snap out of it," I said, clapping my hands and breaking through the cocoon of his coagulated social lethargy: "be friendly, be more social." He looked dazed. "What for?" he growled, obviously incurable.

I wondered whether it was a girl. "Could be," I decided. "Any love problems?" I shouted. "Why, no. Why?" "Just wondering," I said, and cursed myself.

"Money, probably," came my next conclusion. "Short of dough?" I insanely yelled. "Not right now. Why?" "Never mind," I quickly amended, searching the gutters for my briefly misplaced dignity, which only increased my general apprehension of myself as a fool, and a very foolish one at that. I tried one more time.

"Does death worry you?" I pierced the air. "What death? Whose?" I gave up. "Why are you blue?" I screamed. "Blue? Who? Who are you calling blue?" This clowned my tragedy, crowned my triumph, and an immense absurdity quite overtook me, and I became so ridiculous as to be almost sublime in my new role. As a change of pace, and to drown my emotions, I knelt down, pierced my tear-hole, and abandoned myself to sob after sob, until I had thoroughly wept. "What's the matter?" my friend's concerned note broke in. "A mood, a passing mood," I explained. He looked puzzled, and I could see him stretching every mental muscle and tensing his total sympathetic fibre, to strike an understanding pose, a nerve of empathy that would unlock the interpersonal floodgates and unleash the centuries-pent sea of forgotten pity.

"I'm sorry for you," he said. Embracing him, I added, "And I for you." Ah, we were love-brothers.

* * *

All at once, barely stopping to explain himself, my friend grew awkwardly silent. I woke up, pursuing my breath until I had sneezed. This transition, from a state of near-bliss to one of missbliss, profoundly ruined a thought that I had just been about to think. It was a dream grown cold. "Why did you go to sleep, damn you. Didn't you know I was talking to you?" These were my friend's unkind words, and I knew, almost instinctively, that he was in a wounded mood. "I fell asleep to flatter you. That way I can never contradict your opinion." Instead of soothing him, this explanation aroused his further wrath. He made a big bulging fist, and plunged it against me. It was full of inside knuckles, and the bones stabbed me where it hurt. "I feel a whole lot better," he immediately confessed: "Somehow your pain is a balm on my own shattered nerves."

Now we were so even, neither owing or being owed to by the other, that a neutral calm grew up between us. The agonizing suspense hovered over us both. The air literally screamed, so supercharged was it with the dynamic excess of two friends' total composite of ennui.

Gradually, it grew from monotonous to just plain boring. This provoked my friend to fall asleep, and while he was asleep, he fell asleep again, without bothering to wake up to do so. This showed intense concentration. He slept like two men. Or rather, like a man and a woman, since they are one.

To keep tip a steady contrast between us, I remained awake. Gradually, the contrast took on bizarre proportions, he being the essence of asleep, and I the epitome, the living true heart, of sheer pure wakefulness.

But life brings change. Life caused him to wake up. At the very moment, I began to submerge into a drowsy state. So we passed each other, like two ships traveling in opposite directions. The crew and some passengers waved from the railing, and that was it.

He had left a dream wide open for me, so I simply settled into it. The beginning was his, of course, but the ending was typically mine. Now that I remember, I forget it.

Once in a while, we were both awake simultaneously. But this fact brewed many wars, and scrutinizingly we avoided it.

Once there was a violent transaction. He awoke and I fell asleep at the identical time. It was normal to exchange greetings. Falling asleep, I said "Hell—," and waking, he completed it with "—o." Thus it took our double effort to compose one salutation.

This share-the-labor plan, which works well in governments and economies, by dividing up work and letting each member specialize, suited my friend's personality; and as for mine, since at the time I was utterly devoid of even a remote one—I'm referring to a personality— anything would have delighted or dismayed me, it makes no difference.

* * *

Enabling me to practice my vanity, a mirror withstood my steadiest gaze. After studying my character inside out, I concluded that I was deficient in personality. This, more than most anything, added to my self-mal-consciousness. By way of atoning, I applied to my friend, who at that moment had more of himself than even he knew how to deal with. "May I borrow," I asked, "part of the personality you're not using tonight?" "It depends," he answered, a note of suspicion interfering with what might have been generosity had he ever acquired it for a trait; "But why?" "I have a date," I explained, "and am anxious to make the most bombarding impression possible on her nerves. This might awaken her interest."

But he loaned me a disgusting personality, which he always kept in his basement in case a sour enemy approached. I donned the personality, and the girl I dated rejected me after our first few seconds. No sooner she saw me coming through the door, my face, manner, and attitude soaked through and through to the bone with my secondhand character defect, then a moral nausea putrefied her welcome and made her acid tongue proclaim: "If you don't turn around and go I'll call a priest—or a social investigator, at the very least." Then she shut the door, catching one of my legs in the bargain. I was about to pull away and leave it behind, when the door opened to allow me the totality and a half that I had come with. Thus crippled in ill-matched abundance, I ran a rapid limp and found my friend practicing oneness with his spare parts. "Here, I don't need it anymore," and I ripped off the vile qualities and dropped them at his feet. They hung their head in shame in facing their rightful owner, like a banker's daughters returning from a brief bout of prostitution. He refused to claim them, and, lacking the moral worth to qualify tears, these offsprings of a discarded personality organized a stink protest. We closed the windows, fearing that religion would be undermined. Little children, with their personalities yet unborn, were walking outside. How unnecessary to contaminate the young generation, those pure breeders of future malice. My friend pinched in his nostrils, to ward off evil. The ugly personality lay like a corpse between us, its breath barking out a concerted odor of decay. My friend was worried for his human dignity. I, having abandoned mine long ago, was concerned with mere unpleasantness. We poured stale men's perfume and underarm bath destinkeroo on that disembodied batch of pathopsychology below. I don't wish this personality on anyone, not even my most suicidal enemy. It was a compound of the worst germs, featuring vanity, dishonesty, and you name it. My friend disowned it entirely. I remembered the girlfriend's reaction, and found it hard put to blame her. Certainly Hell was devised for no better purpose than to serve as an off-limits cemetery to safekeep these radioactive germs from human intoxication. Finally a welfare collector came in with a disinfected face and whisked away the corpse. This was a splendid public service.

My friend was now smiling. Craving some clean purity, he popped open every window, inhaling keen delight from the very sky. By one of those coincidences that are only allowed to occur in literature, spring happened along. Leaves, plants, and grass, though low in nature's order, are devoid of many flaws native to King Man's personality, so we received them with unfeigned courtesy. My friend plucked a new leaf, and vowed he would turn it over. I went home to the mirror, and virtue blazed a hole in the glass, rounding out an otherwise uneventful personality.

* * *

Carefully alone, and raging with my narcissism, I paid my mirror a courtly visit, pompously expecting a view glorious to myself in the role of image. Not being handsomely rewarded, I sulked and pouted, which worsened the reproduction, and repainted the original in a graver version. When but at that moment should my friend inevitably appear? "Did you distort that mirror?" I accused. "No, Ugly, it was all you," he replied, overlapping my venom. "Don't you blame it on me, damn you," I said, and with a good kick cracked our image off that unlucky mirror. While this disaster was taking place, my friend, using his sense of timing, disappeared. "Come back, coward, it was you," I called, and from afar I could hear, "Glass is sticking to my eyes, help me to locate an oculist quick, I—." Then the voice seemed to faint. With the mirror in disrepair now, and my friend blindly absent from his veto or testimony, my good looks felt safe to appear, and made an instant hit on the scene. They even almost looked like me, except for a sneaking resemblance to my friend. Whose absence is never more present, and vainly spoils my solitude.

* * *

"I bore myself," my friend said. "That's funny," I answered, "I do too." So we tried boring each other. The result was a double bore. "You don't entertain me," I told him. "Go consult your own mirror," he said, and walked a vague distance away. "And multiply myself?" I asked, but he pretended not to hear. "This fat world is one big dirty mirror," I said, and my friend's answer sailed over the clear evening air: "Then go look in it, you slob." "Why?" I asked. "Because you deserve it." "And you, you're so marvelous yourself?" I lashed at him—"You're just a sick disgusting fool." He looked at me belligerently. A double edged mirror intervened.

Infuriated, his curse bounced back at him. Ditto mine. The torture grew so severe that as a last resort we made friends.

* * *

Shadow boxing for fun and exercise, I hit my friend with a well-aimed blow, which severed us by its impact. "Don't be afraid of my shadow," I warned him in apology. "Then do your practicing on a cloudy day," he cowered, "or with the electric light out." "Then how can I see what I do?" I asked, trying to be logical at the same time. The sun gave me more shadow, covering him completely. "Where are you," I asked, lighting a candle. "In the dark," came his faraway voice. "What dark?" I asked. "Come find me," he said. I did, and struck a lighted match. He rubbed it in. "Revenge," he shrugged. "You're cruel," I replied. "Naturally," he gladdened. The sun went out. So did fire, and light. I blackened. My senses abandoned me, and joined the enemy camp. He claimed them, gleefully. "Traitors, deserters," he said, and treated them like honorable spies. What an enemy. I only hate him. So why must he hurt me? It isn't fair. I must find out. Reviving, I slaughtered him. He, in retaliation, simply annihilated me. What friendly competition.

* * *

"Have you become my enemy?" I asked my friend. "I'm always your enemy," he replied, "otherwise nature would never have grouped us." I took out my salt shaker to pour his words over my shoulder, and then confronted my so-called image in the full length of a mirror. "So that's you," I nodded. "And do I look so different?" my friend replied, taking a familiar liberty. "No, only strange, that's all," I added. He and I smiled together, and let that serve as our bond. "If you're myself," I bewildered, "then who am I?" "You have just echoed my very doubt," he answered, as if that solved anything. To free my mind from the panic of self-questioning, I resolved to be stupid. "That's no cure," he said shrewdly, while I bit our tongue. "Do your own bleeding," he demanded, and strangely left me all by myself.

115

"Which one is you and which one is me?" I asked my friend point-blank. After reflecting somewhat, and with careful deliberation, weighing the pros and cons on the selfsame scale with fact and fiction to appraise scientifically the self-evidence contrary to moral interference on an arbitrary basis of right against wrong, my friend juried his suspension and examined every corner of his legible conscience, gathering clues, irrelevancies, and pertinent data to nonsegregationally prosecute severe antidiscrimination, and compiled, verified, authenticated, leaving nothing out and including more than everything in, stuffing the entire universe to overflowing in the answer to my question, it being, "Which? I don't know. You tell me. Someone is right. Maybe. Who knows. Sometimes, anyhow. Why? And why again. Do you doubt? Which is which. Is it relevant? I can't tell. It doesn't matter. What is, or isn't? You or me, which one? Who are you?" Then he stopped, rather for want of breath than a loss in motivational curiosity. "It's hell to be uncertain," I replied, "how about letting a mirror decide, and we'll both put our faces in it at once." "Sure, let's do it," my friend was game. We presented ourself flush face full in the mirror, bombarding that glass by surprise with its guard caught down, scaring, joltifying, shockshaking it, until by embarrassing necessity, or for some other reason certainly outside descriptive nature, it gave us back a definite image, a solid image—one face. "Is it yours or mine?" we both heard ourselves say, so simply simultaneously that only one of us was a person, and the other had to be a full spook. So we suspected each other, and while deeply involved in mutual suspicion we ignorantly failed to notice that in the mirror—that eloquent trouble-source—the whole face was featured by a grin; a grin so totally impersonal as to almost disfigure that one boundless face. If we had seen it, who knows?, but our dispute would have found its certain solution, beyond which even compromise falls redundantly absurd. But we failed to see it, and missed our lifetime chance. Doubt splits us, like paradise lost, or withheld, due to that ignorant fatal apple, knowledge. Or maybe we were just plain stupid. Our splendid revenge, providentially merciless, was to be glued and superimposed to each other for the remainder of time's double duration, concealing identity until even identity couldn't identify itself, but could only exist—or pretend to—by rumor, hearsay, chance conjecture, hunch, problematical doubt, potluck, accident, fortune, superstition, games, cards, dice, the occult formation of stars against mystery's heaven, word of mouth, play-by-ear, improvisation, self-nose-following, weirdities, oddities, strange abnormalities, toys of the wind, washed away sand, tides of chance and flows of the unknown. Who are we? That question answers itself, by splitting the vote directly down the line, and giving us two noes. In this modern age, yes is very unfashionable, and never dares put in an appearance unless disguised by no, or something equivalent. My friend and I were puzzled, but that didn't stop us from being wrong. Being wrong is everyone's universal prerogative, backed by constitutional law, and is fully exercised in the spirit of freedom. For this we live.

* * *

No use speculating on whether my friend was once born, when quite evidently he's at least partly alive now. Things had been carried so far, there was no reason to look back. Most people had a past birth, i.e., being born was already behind them, in the important (one might say vital) aspect of Time, as pertaining to life. My friend, however, announced himself dead, rather than born. This was rushing things: the middle separated the start from the finish, and was (I could discern, at an observational point of view) still going on, at the present moment of himself. "Never was I born," he said, "as yet. So death is bored waiting. 'Come along,' it says. So there I am. At last it's nice to be final for a while. Continuity gives me nervous tension of anxiety. What a quiet rest I find, in my pre-born death. Like a vacation before my time: I get hired, but not before the boss gives me a vacation. And why return? And go back to work I never had? So don't disturb me, with your living temptations. Well off is gone enough. Existence is not very satisfactory: death being lacking, creating a vacuum-image of itself in the living life of the person alive. Leave me alone, friend. Isn't death sacred to you?" Then he left off talking, and disappeared through time into the present, there and then visible on the spot. It was, alone, only he; nor was anything else missing that could have contributed to his existence. This made birth seem very likely, as a past event in his life. And made his death immediately improbable, except as an emergency operation if the future should choose to disinherit itself, cut off from the continuing legacy. Was time outside my friend, knocking vainly on the door, and blindly peering in through the window? His living remained the same fact it was, since death taught it its first beginning. How old has he been new, in so remaining a form? When all life got its start, was he around to collect dividends, dying the life through to enter now on his continuous arrival? How incessant of him! The trouble with him is that he can't be confined. Let me narrow him, and handcuff him to local definitions, limiting his unbroken age to the shallow year of his youth. And light up his life, as diffused from death's night. Or is life the night, and death the day, beneath unexcavated rock of outdated history? Come forward, my friend, as you are, and let traits strap you down, here by now. Surely as yourself, emerge, as something lived by death in your borrowed state of condition, decaying your timely rate away from the permanent metaphysics of my questions. Spirit, be longer yet.

"Oh but you're not *really* dead," I said; "only symbolically." "Isn't that enough?" answered the soul through its timeless skull. "Well at least evolution includes you." "Evolution hell," my friend replied: "evolution hasn't even been born yet, compared to how old I am." "But if you're old, haven't you existed?" "You call that existing!" he said, with a fatuous grin. "Then just how old are you?" "Wait till I'm born, louse." "Who are you callin' louse?" I shouted angrily. He laughed himself silly. The laughing is expected to stop about a few hours after Judgment Day, standard time, and *that* I'm willing to wait around for. But first I must begin to wait. So I buy a wristwatch. It's worthwhile to watch the hands go slowly around. Every second brings eternity that much closer. Time is terrific. It improves the memory, it develops our patience, ripens our hope, fulfills our apprehension, and rewards us with two classical consolation prizes: regret and nostalgia. (It's too morbid to include grief.) Yes, I sure am a time fan. I constantly root. I cheer its speed, and boo its breathtaking heartbreaking slow ruinous decay, reducing solid matter to—to something like my friend.

Reading my thought, my friend slugs me. "I insist on existing," he says, with resolution, determination, and a change of heart. "So who's stopping you?" I say meekly, about to collapse. "Surely not you," he taunts, cruel as Survival.

* * *

"Does religion interest you?" I asked my friend. "Yes, it's the most pious topic I know," he prayerfully replied, "and does a whale of a job keeping God in power. But does the Holy One rake in every profit? What about the common man—like us? Have we no share, or stake, no vote, but are kept subservient under the Divine Monarchy?" "That's a very general doubt you just uttered," I said, "but it's theological, as I know your faith is in the right place." "Where?'" he asked, and looked between his legs. To counteract his move, I looked high up, and got sunburnt in the process (despite the rain that day, since indoor electricity has some heat). We searched all over for God, Who eluded us by being everynowhere, all in the same one time. It distracted our attention, which vaguely dissolved in disillusionment, wanting for a focus. God would have been comfortable to believe in, with His almighty and traditional reputation. What an outcast my friend felt like! Fallen from faith, and shorn of all substitute. In this deprived state, he grieved for the devout former eras that would not shake a meditative man from the exalted loftiness of his souls, communicative bliss, to the harsh outer doubts of realistic scepticism, in the lower land below. Well, my friend thought. The more he did so, the more swayed he was to put all his faith in doubt, hoping for a reprieve. How cold is a Godless soul. What lack of ardor! Ah, the boiling negative of my friend! His brain was sufficient unto itself, as a hell to be; bright paradise receded from his view, and heaven lost its image. What remained? Fear's radiant nothing, those beams of darkness. How strikingly unreal, how remote from the terror, love, and light. So sinks my friend, in the deep shallows of the surface. What regret! Oh Joy, return!

My friend was undoubtedly. After a while, he was even more so. By then, it was all he could handle. At last, the strain was too much. Then the crack came. And now, he's doubtfully. Or so he claims, until proven otherwise. He's dizzy with doubt. It gets out of hand. The doubt swells, and becomes a gigantic cancer, swallowing wholesale tissue of ripe sweet truth. Vast doubt, like a dragon whose appetite destroys the harmless dreams of fancy and those difficult facts sweated and bled from the sick body of experience. "What are you so doubtful about?" I asked my friend, who looked faith-fallen. He scanned me suspiciously, shook his shaken head, and said with emphasis, "I have my doubts." "So you do," I approved, and could see the shiny kindly beam of belief dispersing the shadows of negation in those world-blurred eyes, where now sight itself began simply to be renewed, inspired by the blind debt of trust it had to pay to the colossal bank of the unknown. "I see the light," he said, and freely decorated his jaws with what, in normal times, was cracked out to be a smile. "Don't overdo it," I warned. When will innocence and experience, I wondered loosely, stop being divorced and begin to get married?—and bear ideally real children?

"Where's your doubt?" I said. "Buried," my gay friend answered, like heaven having just witnessed hell's funeral. "You're not in mourning?" I chastised. "No, I'm wake now," he overjoyed himself by saying. Back of him, a rare rainbow appeared, fully stocked with an entertaining variety of the complete spectrum of colors, let alone only black and white. "There it is," I said. He turned. It shattered his incredulity, like sparks of atoms showering into every rotating direction of circular possibility. "I'm thrilled," said my friend, after silence had chilled his response. "I'm quite glad for you," I said, calmly within bounds. "Don't you believe me?" he implored, with wrinkles of alarm upsetting the purity of his face. "Oh undoubtedly," I callously replied. By then, my poor friend lacked a heart to support a further answer. He wrapped himself in silence, and found comfort in his old enemy, despair. I felt left out. But since his sullen mood suited him, I graciously gave way.

"I'm not brooding anymore," he declared. "That's excellent," I said: "let's celebrate." So we got drunk. Then we got high. Then we lost our soberness. And finally, finishing the bottle, we were only too sober. This completed our doubt.

* * *

My friend, and I too, have been through a lot. Despite the phases of our various experiences, we wonder even more vaguely than before what the whole thing is all about. Conceptual theories serve no good: We're ripe to permanently be actual on the dawn of the real.

After all, what is reality? We've about run the gamut. Religious insight, mystical revelation, tragic renunciation, diabolical despair, and the infernal chamber of lowest pessimism, have been invoked to melody and flourish on the versatile instrument of our life, but what theme is musically supreme, to which all others must play a subordinate tune? Plagued by purpose, we dispelled our impatience, put away our immunity, and declared ourselves ripe for whatever revelation reality chose fit as a declaration in deed and intent of its total intrinsic self. Come what may. We would midwife the visitation, and so fly on the wings of birth. Oh now, if ever.

"Demonstrate the presence of reality," I dared my friend. "Oh, it declares itself," he said, and we stood by waiting for it to happen. Time went by, that's all. After the silent interval had been prolonged to no purpose, my friend suddenly declared, "We're it! We're the reality."

"Can you prove it, can you prove it, can it be done?" I asked, with my life at stake and so out at the end of my rope that one more inch would hang me.

"Take me for example," my friend offered, like a guinea pig sacrificing himself for a scientific experiment; "let me draw the complete circle, and describe the cycles of my round life, making both ends meet to justify a drawn-out middle—or muddle, I should say. But I won't apologize. This is me, in realism. Here's what I do, and the reality it causes, or is, because I'm the doer or I'm the thing that's done. Or being done, daily and nightly, formed until a moment brings a beginning to formlessness and draws me outside my own circle of self on a basis of timeless forever:

"Whenever I think, a thought turns up. For this, I have my brain to thank.

"After the thought is over, I act. This keeps me practical.

"After I act, I repent. This is where God comes in.

"Then, I rebel. Atheism takes over, to justify my instinctive behavior.

"When society intervenes, I compromise by falling in love.

"If condemned to marriage, I wheel a baby carriage. If not, I become a poet.

"In the end, death knows just where to find me. I hide behind my falling skin."

"Do you stand by what you say?" I asked. By way of answer, he began his forward fall.

* * *

"I wonder what life means," said my friend when he had apparently just been thinking. "I have no idea," I volunteered in my cheerful manner, helpful and yet lighthearted at the same time; for philosophy was to me both an agreeable and an instructive science and presented many worthwhile topics of significance and entertainment to the whole world, and would be a useful ornament rather than a disgrace in any adult conversation that claims to be mature and reflect these enlightened modern times, when so many human beings have received a college education that illiterate democracy is simply packed solid with an unprecedented quantity of well-rounded cultural ingredients, much to the united pride of this abounding twentieth-century intellect.

"Then is life empty?" my friend wondered, and grew very serious. His face was so completely devoid of a smile, it puzzled me just where the smile could be concealed, in what drawer or shelf of his emotion-littered, response-stocked, act-filled self, where the rubbish of life's used-up necessities was casually discarded and haphazardly left to accumulate. "Of course not," I answered, and propriety allowed me to be shocked, which properly checked my negative friend's implied impiety.

"Is it good, true, and beautiful?" he asked, borrowing those terms from heaven or some other spiritual source, because facts derived from experience left at most a vague impression or scrawny impact on what psychiatrists were pleased to commonly refer to as his "mind." "Yes, naturally," I replied. "I'm glad," he said, "and I feel much better, and will conduct my life accordingly." From then on, I avoided him.

But he found me. "You're wrong," he said, exposing his smile to the sunlit air as a general would air his bravest medal to a heroic military assemblage in the brassy hour and strained glory of his defeated nation's formal ceremonies of surrender, acclaimed by standards on high and the deflated notes of a bugle. "Well, I'm sorry for you," I said, and excused myself with protests of apology, claiming a prior appointment. "You rat," he called after me, while embarrassment plugged up my ears with that convenient social nicety, deafness.

Next day's accident made us meet again. "It stinks," said my friend, referring to that scapegoat of our abstract misery, life. I took my stand: "Not necessarily," I wisely cautioned. "Oh moderate, are you?" cracked my friend, and rolled up all his anger in one extreme smile, from which it is likely I shall never recover as long as life remains as a full-time participant in the mechanical operations and worldly transactions of that well-established and traditional firm, my soul-sponsored body.

* * *

Everything my friend does is in vain. He even fails in vain. "I guess no one is perfect," said my friend, and by that he meant himself, if only the truth be known. He universally applies himself. If he's thirsty, he says, "That moon is thirsty." Can you blame it, then, when the moon reports drunk?

Or if my friend should happen to kiss a girl, and the girl isn't there at the time, he kisses her anyway. It doesn't hurt.

Or whenever money is involved, my friend participates in every way except what really counts: possession. Possession doesn't agree with him. He's not even self-possessed. As a remedy, he does without. This drains his resources, and eats up all his working capital.

In the long run, he's due to die. But he keeps putting it off, laying months aside, even years, for future use. He saves. Saves continually, and draws interest.

"What am I here for?" he says at last. There's no answer, but he agrees with it.

* * *

My friend is completely democratic. He hates all men alike. He has a white hatred for a white man, a black hatred for a colored man. His equality is

123

so neutral, his hate is as weak as love, and doesn't do anything except live the idle life of an emotion. Elsewhere, my friend's behavior is another thing. It's full of conduct and activity. All his busy-ness is centered there. It's the seat of accomplishment, but theory aside it's all a practical waste. No sooner was the last foot out of the womb when the first foot is sinking into the tomb. In the span between, my friend has succeeded in leaving a vacuum as empty as he found it. This is good manners, as hollowness goes. His death is sure to be democratic. He'll probably vote. For the defeated candidate, after it happens. That poor little one-man walking minority, will he ever be effectual? Not likely, I tell you. His mind is too many-sided, without being anywhere. Decisions frighten him, so he decides to avoid them. They feel mutual about it, and steer clear, absolving all commerce with his uncertain mind, and his rather rackety brain. He, he doesn't know what to do. He just stands around. "It's gentlemanly to be undecided," he says, "and indicates a certain refinement. Either in me, or in my hesitating thoughts. I can't tell which. All I want is peace: I'll consent, and agree with anything. Even with ideas, if possible. I aim to accommodate, and please. You up there," (looking at his ideas) "please note: anything you do is all right. Go ahead. I won't mind."

Ideas have a mind of their own, so my friend thinks twice before contradicting his ideas. His own mind, however, is often changed. One thing my friend is not: stubborn.

No, he wouldn't think of being stubborn, because he's too stubbornly thinking. Acts are another thing. Thoughts do his acting for him, or acts his thinking, and make him a well-rounded misfit. He's a product of his own application, but all too frequently assumes the minor role of byproduct. Selling himself short, he does. But he does the buying, anyway. Either way, it's a costly deal. But cheap.

The mind of my friend is preoccupied with thought, and has no behavior to think of. My friend himself must act, but lacking an active brain he manages to scrape by on nerves. Back there, in the thought-flooded room, the mind keeps aloof from the stupidity and absentmindedness by which my friend's conduct gains some consistency.

By the way, does my friend use facts, or have any use for them? Or is he too practical, and too matter-of-fact? No, the contrary: Though useless for utility, facts are a futility strikingly beautiful and superbly abstract. It's a case of pure art, for its own sake of deep warmhearted love, excluding the money factor.

Facts were always extremely interesting for my friend. However, he never uses them for his thinking, since they spoil his theories. So he appreciates them abstractly, as though they were non-objective works of art, and applies his practical everyday business to the independent functioning of his mind. He purifies the mind daily, dusting the corners to wash away every speck of fact. Then, full of vacuum and fantasy, he's ready to take decisive act.

Act? Positively. Action brings out the active side in him, which, in his characteristic ruggedness, he's ready to exploit. The beast.

"I'm very practical," my friend will always frankly admit. How right. Even his dreams are practical, and his ideals are so practical he's always wasting his life trying to apply them, making absurd and foolhardy attempts to give them suitable application and convert them to reality. It never works.

One day, he idealized a girl. Being a man of action, he was very practical. But her answer was "no."

Then he had another ideal: money. But he was too practical to work for it. Being practical, he got results: near-starvation. He's never without his results. He'd feel naked without them.

Even his thoughts are practical. Which is poetic justice, I think.

"You're damn mental, aren't you?" I asked him, "and not only that, but worse, you're even subjective," I accused him, sort of viciously, it hurts me to confess. He admitted it. "Explain your mind!" I confronted him, and blocked off all exits, which drove him dreadfully into himself. He's still there, I believe. Sort of frightened, and thinking at the same time. "I once experienced unexpected surprise," he informed me at length, and continued, in a schizophrenic tone, which brought insanity into the picture, like a wholesome breath of clean air. "The couch!" I pointed. He lay there, expostulating with his other self in a well-modulated monotone so catatonic I morbidly dozed off into our collective unconscious, pursuing the archetype of forbidden dreams, until with a start I woke up while he was still beginning, like a blind man's vague feeble gestures groping against a solid wall to step over the stumbling block of a protracted threshold, and making slow dreamlike progress in a backward delirium toward the black room he has just emerged from, halting and hesitant, just the sort of man the Kingdom of Heaven was built for, he being meek and having been inherited by a reluctant earth, although the lawyer's will was contested. His interminable words, spaced far into the recess of time, follow, approximately, with a fair degree of originally reproduced accuracy and faithfulness to the carbon copy:

"Once I was standing on the front of my toes, watching the wind curl westward, lurching with the uneven distribution of my past, and slowly contaminating the air by passing it through my breath. Many current events were confronting the world, such as the stuff that headlines feed on, but I was distracted by an internal outburst of surprise. This surprise was without an object, and so caught me totally unprepared. I was almost about to say something, but then thought better of it. My eyes expressed contrary emotions, but no compromise was in sight. Temporarily blinded by this hesitation, I directed the confusion upward, where my brain was in session. 'What, another thought!' it proclaimed. My arms and legs sat waiting on nerves, hoping for an act. 'The mentality of everything!' something in me said, and when I turned around the experience had vanished behind me."

"Do you miss it?" I asked, touched. "Sometimes," he said; "but thought is everything." I took him at word value, full face, salting him a grain. He even makes love with his mind. He has a virile brain. God, look at that solid muscle!

My friend is very mental. Even his muscles are mental. Only his brain is physical. But his arms, legs, and other parts of his body are strictly platonic. A girl found this out. Trapped between my friend and a bed,

126

with no air dividing the three, she was confined to pure, abstract, and absurdly ideal love. Now her belly is swollen with an enormous idea, which threatens at any day to become an emotion. This will cause my friend to become an intellectual father. To prepare for this cozy event, his muscles are taking genius lessons, and his entire body, without a single exception, is creatively in a library.

* * *

Drink and my friend don't mix. But to my error, I mix too often with him then. Down go our drinks, and high pop up we. Later, our immoderation so weakens me, his sadism is irresistible to us both, in our alcoholic cooperation.

"Say when," I said, pouring a drink. He didn't, so it spilled over the brim. "Clod!" I remarked, lapping the excess from the spongy tablecloth. Then, from brim to bottom of glass, he did justice to the remainder. "A little social drinking," he burbled, "never did—" (After vomiting, he continued) "harm to nobody." Then he repeated the performance. Drenched with his spew, I lapped up its alcoholic content, and we sang a few Christmas carols (though it was early summer probably, give or take half a year, no doubt). "Say when," he gushed, spilling a bottle down my throat. When it reached the brim of my lips, I choked incoherently, drowned in clean fun. "This is living," I managed to utter, at great length, and he generously agreed with me. Urging our willpower to the breaking point, we resisted the temptation to be moderate. "That stuff is for the Greeks," we agreed (meaning moderation). Triumphing our minds over matter, we drank a rejoicing toast, and declined into a stupor. We no longer felt bored.

To avoid a hangover, we decided to drink. I mildly hesitated: "Shouldn't we pause a bit?" wisdom prompted me to ask. His face clouded. "In the world, why?" he promptly enquired. "Between drinks is like an author between novels: pausing for inspiration." "That's bunk," he declared, and drank himself blue. I followed suit, but overdid it. He stopped and fell asleep. I kept going, the night through, to ache my life's pain out of me with this soothing interior of wipeaway ointment. By repeating this liquid movement, I was soon close to sober, and to cure this stubborn evasion I clobbered on with a renewal of more drinking, so that pleasure might somewhat substitute for its familiar opposite, mankind's famous enemy. Thus I drank, from a humane cause, a motive of unexampled dignity. How I outparalleled my friend, in the disciplined rapture of untamed abandonment. Notably, I was he, which he wouldn't regret, when the consequences fell in my name. He only helped me to them.

Nerve endings give me a pain, so I rolled my sober self into a compact ball and dropped it whole into a glass, displacing the momentary whiskey. Then, when my smile reappeared at my nape, and walking increased my distance to the destination, I felt at remote cousinship to my old enemy, pain. Like a cue, my friend reared his ugly head. "Are you staggering?" he asked, with his judgment askance. "No, but the world is," I replied, heeding the first scapegoat that had the courtesy to offer itself. (The world winced, but remained calm.) Meanwhile, my elbows were privately scratching each other, for a reason mysterious to this very day. Also, my knees were not operating properly, but I was too busy to find out just what bothered them. My friend propped me up on a vertical bed, but the helium-filled pillow kept itself lifted from the comfort of my head, giving me the incentive to fall down, which I did (a man of action doesn't waste time on rhetoric). Of course, I screamed in advance, so the debt of pain was paid off before the bill was forwarded. This afforded me, in reverse, a kind of pleasure familiar to masochists. Not being dead, I felt a strong urge for life. The compromise, of course, was a coma.

Easter reawakened me, along with other species of flowers. When the bees went pollen hunting in my dense armpits, I felt the glorious sting of nature, and revived totally. I leapt out of bed, eager for an amorous adventure. But first I had to call up for a date. But the telephone operator turned me down.

Then I looked for a pickup. All I heard was "How dare you?" This interfered with my success.

Later, I met my friend. "This is my blind date," and he introduced us. The seeing-eye dog growled at me. "Has she a friend?" I asked. So it was arranged for that night. After grooming my hair and polishing my skin, I dressed with careful distaste in front of the mirror, and picked her a flower from the park when I went to her house. She proved easy to handle, thanks to the leash.

Early the next morning, in fact before I woke up, I drank unintentional urine from an intentional bottle of alcohol. This was my friend's silly little joke.

And hard to ignore. He smiled benignly, and offered to prepare an edible antidote to dissipate the yellow taste from the sour hole at whose opening my food and drink gets poured. But the food he concocted was pure poison, and itself required a purgative. Thus his favor was really harm, and as he went to sleep death stood waiting for me, tempting my slightest weakness. I felt, indeed, horrible. Under the circumstances, why not? I'm very adaptable.

After eating myself to death, I vomited life out again, and remained to recuperate. First I mixed equal portions of wine, beer, and milk, held my nose by proxy, and drank the compound much to the confusion of my eighty or ninety senses. When the effect wore off, I reawoke like Rip Van Winkle, and after tripping on my beard, I searched out the skies ('twas night) for the latest eternal gossip. A meteor flashed, and I immediately recognized my century. While groping for the nearest comet, I sprained my rheumatism again, and the comic effect held me dripping in laughter.

Aroused from sleep, my friend madly dashed to the rescue. Gradually my convulsions lessened. He poured some pepper in my mouth, and let my sneeze ease out through one of my ears (I forget the other). This restored me to my youth.

"How are you?" he asked. The *faux pas* gently prodded me to a relapse.

Here is a faithful approximate exact recording of a conversation between me (patient) and him (hospital visitor) while I was convalescing from my convalescence:

"Are you better?" he asked. (I winced.)

"Is there anything I can do?" (With my nether eye, I indicated the exit door, but he was too concerned with my recovery to hurry after the cue.)

"Have you been swallowing your medicine?" (For answer, I displayed my tongue, where several holes were in evidence, to show just where the medicine went through. His practiced eye also saw several symptoms, but his civil tongue kept a quiet score on that account.) I settled my pillow into a more comfortable arrangement, and searching within one of the folds, found my head again. As usual, it was diminishing with maluse. Batting my eyelashes for exercise, to my horror I found the nurse responding to a wink, or flirtation. "Three's a crowd," shouted my friend, and he disappeared.

Bruised by a kiss, I asked the nurse for weak tea. Hard of hearing, she immediately unfurled her breast. "No!" I shouted, while sorrow sprinkled from her eyes. "Are you a mother?" "Not yet," she managed, catching her breath. "Well don't practice on me," I yelled.

Thus frustrated, she bled me through an exposed artery, timed my loss of consciousness, and promptly saved my life by summoning a convenient doctor. With a deathless bedside air, full of grace and diplomacy, and wearing a grey moustache, he introduced some vitamins to my system and, being a Christian Scientist, began to pray. This unlikely combination resurrected me. I tipped him (it was my last nickel) and began to plan my afterlife.

As I hobbled away from the hospital, who should I meet but my friend? "Are you all right," he said, with frantic emphasis. It was with the greatest difficulty, and deep regret, that I had to tell him no.

* * *

Here's my friend, reminiscing about his faraway origin:

"An amoeba gave me birth. Don't ask me when.

"When my mother split up with herself, my loyalty became divided.

"Once launched, I roared through evolution. At one time, I was considered the perfect missing link. But I escaped, and made further progress.

"Historians romp through caves, searching for me. Antiquaries dig for my seedless bones with their spineless shovels and with spades, rakes, and hoes numerous as a golf pro's clubs. But I merely grow more ancient, while time renews itself daily.

"Every time I kiss a girl, evolution jumps backward two paces. By the time we embrace, Darwin is waking up again, and prehistoric dawn sighs against the void of the world.

"I think often of my mother, the amoeba. She was conservative by instinct, and psychoanalysis has persuaded me to forgive her. Poor lady. She was sexy, too. How she could split! A ballerina, like. I don't take after her. I'm only male. At least, that's what the psychiatrist told me. And he's paid to be believed. My mother paid. Out of what? Who knows? Herself, maybe. We all do, you know."

"You were psychoanalyzed then?" I smiled. "Yes, in the womb," he answered: "The analyst charged my mother one price for us both. My mother was far too neurotic to resist such a tempting bargain. So you see, I was cured before I was born." "Are you still cured?" I asked. "No. Today is another day. One grows up, you realize. Now I'm *maturely* neurotic, an event my mother never anticipated when she underwent womb treatment." "Where is she now?" I gently hinted. "Back where I've got to follow once I've gone far enough to reverse life's road back to its predestination." "You're obscure," I complained. "Not yet," he promised.

* * *

I'm afraid my friend is crazy. He resists it, when he can. He's never *overtly* crazy, but it's an inner mental condition, and since his insanity is purely psychosomatic, my friend has the heartlessness to politely ignore it when conditions permit. Actually, his personality is so split that if he walks one way his shadow walks the other—foreshadowing some disturbance of the mind. But only on a sunny day can this contrast shine into selective black to play off against the hallucinary white. He plays it cute that way, hedging himself into a neutral middle position and blanking out against accusations, while the pursued paranoia chases itself outside the deranged disorder of his purely involuntary mind, whose conscious drives are so steeped in the unconscious that both his id and libido are caught in the simultaneous act of deathly making love, while the ego tears out its hair and the saintly superego is praying and pulling out all its rosary beads, like a daisy chain, saying, "It loves me, it loves me not," and so forth. Who "it" is, I don't know. Probably some moral agent.

"Talk it out," I said, seeing my friend's disturbance. "May I use free association?" he asked. "Only where you see fit," I restricted, "and let your wisdom judge." He had none. But that's beside the point.

"My body conflicts with my mind," my friend began, on that double note. "Oh, you're kidding!" I said. He only smiled. "Then tell how," I invited. My friend was only too willing to:

"My body does what it wants. My mind applauds or boos, but remains a spectator.

"When my body is sleepy, my mind tends to follow the leader. Soon they sleep side by side, like a husband and his slightly used up wife.

"Sometimes my body wakes, but my mind waits half the day before it discovers its cue.

"Sometimes my mind sees itself in its own mirror, and becomes absorbed for hours. This tireless game, privately played in the dressing room, empties the stands of spectators of my body's customary and artless performance.

"When my mind is neurotic, my body's rhythm is slightly impeded. It will stammer, or find occasion to limp. This, in turn, increases the neurosis of the mind. One frequently attempted solution, of course, is insanity. But one should resort to it only in an emergency, since it is known to be habit forming."

"Then surely *you're* not in danger," I advised. "Why?" "Because you're not addicted to habit—not habitually, I don't think." "I only wish my craziness could be regulated by habit," he moped; "but it breaks out, and has no formula." "Then make *up* a formula," my solution decreed, settling his confusion into one unsavory lump. He shook what went for a head, and declined, as nuisance tampering, my resolve to join his body's union with the mind and so split the mating maladjustment between his originality and the insanity it clings to. "What I am is too much already, so leave me alone," he concluded. The brute brought along his own solitude to brood in. Foreignly outside, I felt my interference fading.

Governed by his odd being, his acts were determined to justify their lack of a system. Even his foolhardiness whipped up integrity's spectacle to morally edify me. Braving a clown identity, my friend stood on his collapsing self.

* * *

My friend has a mental disorder. But in moderation, so it hasn't gone to his head. Only his behavior is crazy, but otherwise my friend has only too much sanity. He puts some away for a rainy day, and invests the rest in good old normality. This is the psychology of his life, and his emotions are absolutely violent on the subject, and would blow their top were it not for his extreme inhibition. As for my friend himself, he's really someone else. That's why the Mental Health Correction Commission never recognizes him. "Incognito," he's classified, which is like being 4F in the army. Daft, but no draft. Neat dodge, heh? My exempt friend, who's disentitled to his own malady on grounds of not being present when most of his symptoms are afflicting him. He takes the non-responsibility for his participations, and claims credit for what he's an outsider to. Rules neither faze nor dismay him, but are overlooked as a duty to the principle of expedience and a concession to the rigors of convenience. Every time he wins, anarchy has to tolerate its moral victory. While amorality celebrates its harsh reign. Institutionalism and established conventions are strictly without his consent, and in spite of his lenient oblivion to their stupendous works. When he dies, the world as presently instituted will go on being not supported by him. This is his vital role in history.

* * *

The world was sad, and my friend decreed an order for fun, or laughter. To be carried out immediately, in effect once his sign has been given. This was very strict. My friend really meant it. "When I laugh," he said, "I want the world to laugh. I want to be confirmed. When I laugh, something funny has been created. I want everyone to agree with me, or I'll be very stern, and have to resort to unfair means. Whoever isn't able to laugh has to go to an institution. This is imperative. I said so, I willed it, so I'm right. As emperor, I order the world to change. My word is magic. The world had better note. My laugh is now officially beginning. When it rises to a peak, I want results, and justification. I don't intend to waste my breath. Here goes. You will change now, world! Or pay, and so change the hard way. Your master has spoken. I am setting a worldly example. Sanity must conform, or be ruled insane at once. Imitate me, damn you! What's inside me is true, is real. And anything that's not is false, is bad. Don't you see? Now, watch me! See my face: it has remade the world, for humor or for death. May this tragic mask be comical, forever."

My friend applied a grin to his face, where it schooled itself with patient homework and graduated in the role of a mature laugh, complete with internal sound effect. Served by this fair warning, the world grew humorous at once, recreating incidents in harmony with the emotional scheme indulged by my friend's laughter. But other people, caught in this sudden turn of events, were thrown into maladjustment by their inadequate preparation in the arts of mirth and the various healing skills of homefashioned practical levity. Unable to adapt themselves to this changed environment, these outmoded victims of their own somberness were herded into the shock departments of mental wards, where benign executioners administered helpless doses of laughing gas. Immediately, the patients excelled in wit, and spoke pun language like a native. Their brains unhatched schemes of original jokes, which provoked such merriment that several overcured diehards rolled over and plunged into the suicide of extreme laughter, which split their sides and scattered their ribs. Meanwhile, my friend lost his smile, and the outside world took on its usual solemnity, in fact overdoing the gloomy bit. This released the mental captives from the madhouse, where discarded frivolity and hasty corpses littered the ashes of the dwindling fumes. A serious doom afflicted the world. My friend grew a grave face, and lingered in his sad business of living.

* * *

My friend and I decided to go. After packing ourselves in a portable trunk, we purchased a tiny ticket through some breathing holes, and boarding a likely vehicle, proceeded to be driven express. When our destination had been more than reached, a stranger undid the public key to our private trunk, and my friend fell out, chased by a wild civil war waged between his knees and elbows. I rolled out, like a carpet displaying itself in the absence of a salesman. "Where are we?" my friend was soon to ask. I politely ignored his unkind question, and set myself to the task at hand: an adjustment to my environment. The environment, however, could not acclimate itself to my adjustment, and, despite hasty guidance by native social workers, was soon throbbing with neurosis. The trees wilted under the wind, houses railed at imaginary mountains, grass barked at citizens, sky froze back its rain, women acted unmarried with their own strange husbands, and children grew younger, falling steadily from their height in a backward chaos that bit the kindly hand of father time. "You had better unadjust," my friend warned me. "Have I projected this?" I asked, taking note of the psychosomatic ills that had converted the environment into an informal lunatic pit. "You sure have," agreed my friend, and added, "Thank God you don't adjust to me." Saying this, he walked away, and before I could scream he had gone straight to the environment. A mad silence paused in my alarm. A minute later, he returned, his features disfigured with blotches of paranoia. Schizophrenia separated him from his walking digits of feet. A manic-depressive hysteria twisted his tongue through each corkscrewy eye, distorting his usual bland manner with an unpleasant delirium. Behind him, however, the environment was normal again. Trees were themselves, wind behaved, houses solidified, children grew up instead of down, rain felt perfectly free to fall, grass took no thought at being green, and husbands wived their women in a licentious outburst of domestic fidelity. "You look out of sorts," I told my friend. "Adjustment troubles," he answered.

* * *

My friend had a stream of consciousness. It embarrassed him. He tried to turn it off, but it rambled on underground, churning up half-nude guilts and stray sins, bargains from black markets and forbidden basements that trade in doubtful pawnful items and stolen sweets. So many households had at least one television set, my friend feared exposure;

those obscene scenes would become a public scandal. Perhaps some shortwave hookup was already providing a channel with mirth, not to mention shock, from the Grade B hellpile that littered the stream of consciousness with inflammable carnal dungheaps of rot and mud. All because of Freud!

My friend went to a psychiatrist quick as possible. "Hurry up, cure me," he said. "You want me to analyze you?" said the doctor between the sausages of his German accent. "Why not?" agreed my friend, turning social. So my friend climbed on a couch and floated away in a dream, while the doctor read *Faust* aloud with mumbling lips.

My friend woke up, full of virgin purity, feeling light as an angel. The doctor was already dead, snoring half-remembered passages from Goethe's masterpiece, the pages of which went up and down on his non-breathing, asthma-ridden, mortality-congested chest. "One hun down the drain," observed my nonpartisan friend.

Where was the stream of consciousness? It was now screened in every church to illustrate a propaganda sermon advocating civilized chastity and godly restraint. Which left my friend empty, and he went out looking for a new emotional life.

He came upon a girl, and they coupled according to instinct. A fresh stream of consciousness was their offspring, which yielded so many criminal tendencies that they had to be repressed. Currently, my friend is insane.

* * *

My friend went to a mental doctor. "Open your mind and say 'Ah,'" said the doctor, who happened also to be blind. My friend was delayed by free association, which interrupted his thought process, but finally the lid lifted from his brain box, revealing some emotions here and there, indulging in harmless domestic pastimes. The doctor groped about, probing severely in the dark with his arthritic hands, until the emotions, like electric bulbs, were blinked out. Then he snapped the case shut, damaging infantile memories. "Now you're in perfect health," he commanded; "go to work, and pay my bill." The office door automatically opened, and a current ejected my friend. An elevator transmitted him to the street. Habit started up his legs, the motor nerves hummed, and walking was done by my friend.

A safety device regulated the crossing of any street where cars and lights threatened his instinctive survival. He adjusted to stimulus with response, performing behavior efficiency at mechanical patterns of organic normality. Needs, conditioning, and motivation functioned at time-space levels of balance, contributing a total integration to his conflict-free personality. He saw me. "Hello" came the word out of his mouth, which his face reinforced with an appropriate smile. Scared, I ran away.

* * *

Nature wouldn't stop to practice birth control, so at its present rate it threatens to continue. My friend violates this rule, due to the absence of death control. Bit by bit, in all sorts of stray ways, he daily dies a little further. He begins to nibble eternity with his brittle and perfunctory teeth, like an obese rodent on a self-imposed diet. His herculean lack of heroism allows him to practice minute-scale vanities with anti-tragic zest. His growth decays into older time, balancing the buoyant hour of his birth. His body has a deeply embedded sensual core, which may explain his addiction to sex. Hunger and other stages of dissatisfaction may be traced back to causes so well-rooted in nature that his universality is practically common.

* * *

My friend succumbed to the blandishments of nature. He went into a public park, and watched a grown-up tree. The sun was doing its best to shine, but its efforts, unseen, were unsung. The day had lots of time, and could easily afford a couple of spare grey hours, especially with an improved average life span giving brighter duration to so many normal human beings. My friend benefited also. He looked at a flower, and observed how delicate it was. A bird caught his eye, but then the sky swung clear around, undoubtedly to dust itself off. When the sky reversed its tumble upright, the bird was nowhere there, perched just outside memory and slipping fast, or flying slightly, into the vast oblivion of my friend.

Once his composure was recovered, and this little incident forgotten, my friend resumed his nonchalance, and strolled this or that way about with one foot lingering just behind the other and then, in a due step course, overtaking it. He fell into the swing of nature. Rhythm of season and plant became his. This loosened his soul, and drove a glory through his thoughts. He narrowed into tiny resistance, while God overcame everything. "What am I, a priest?" he protested, struggling for his release. It was too late to be noble, humble, or whatever the gods ask. Reclaiming himself, my friend saw an utterly banal world. "Home, at last!" he said, with his sweet normality. Trees sagged, and some rain fouled up the sky. The daily week, the monthly year, restored the muddy commonplace in which my friend's well-trained capacity for the inferior instantly rejoiced. "I'll go home and eat," he said.

* * *

My friend tried hard to be human. His success was so vigorous, it almost killed him. One of his first acts of survival, therefore, was to place life at a vast distance, and live it somehow by telepathy. So if a dangerous woman uncoils herself, shredding passion into his nearby air, he abandons the nerves weakly susceptible to her, like a mother discarding her illegitimate children. He starts life anew, like a defeated general with a considerably reduced army, reorganized from the puniest reserves. Experience shrinks him. Like a makeshift boat weathered thin from costly storms, he drops his heavy emotions overboard, resuming the journey with ever lighter ballast and swifter ignorance, toward an unprepared port. Thus he's dimmed precociously into death, which he gyps by having preserved a dearer virginity in the savage market of raw life.

* * *

Nature had an outdoor quality, a freshness, that wore through my friend's sophistication and made him glad all over. In an unguarded moment, he said, "It's beautiful!" This led him to the thought of God, a subject that nourished his entire capacity for ignorance. So he looked at a cluster of trees, from a loving distance, admiring their subdued green in the mist. Then he thought of tragedy, and feared he would die. To reassure himself, he underwent an examination by a doctor schooled in pessimism, with an alarming verdict. By some unfair association, he blamed nature. Now he avoids it whenever possible, and is cultivating sophistication, elegant breeding, and a positive knack for cynicism. Even when he lays on top of a girl, they leave their clothing on and only brief coldness transpires between them, well bred with reserve and dignity. They get up, apologize, and take the separate paths of departure along the paved polish of civilization.

* * *

My friend has become delicately negativist. He's precious and rare, shunning life's dripping sap. Nature's less in him, and decadence more. Some abundant signs, here, analyze the bodily diminishing of his soul.

Since even water is too strong for him, he dilutes it with air in an antiseptic glass, and then, abjuring the coarseness of drinking, he merely smells it. He's even toying with a growing moustache, combing its two hairs and keeping them well perfumed by deliberately inhaling the essence of sunset. Hating exhibitionism, he sneezes internally, and, when his conscience objects, he apologizes profusely. His life hardly has miscalculations, except once he was unavoidably born. He's redeemed that error since. He's wearing gloves and touches nothing but filtered twilight air, which first he sprays with insecticide, to kill off a budding germination of whatever vulgar abundance it's in nature's heart to restore to the crusading return of another annual spring. My friend hates nature. And sex is even worse, he finds. Or refrains from finding. He'll take no chances. Though he believes in history, he'll never practice it. He bleaches his blood, and dines on disinfectant, such as soap. He loves bubbles. Hates them to disappear. Remind him of himself, the transparency of his ways. No death for him, it's too coarse. In advance, he prematurely not lives, as a tribute to his delicacy. It works, too. His bowels are so trained, he simply holds everything in, converts his stomach to an urn, and internally cremates the waste, burning the tedious embarrassment to an ash. As for the ash, it simply comes out through his throat, and is dislodged into his handkerchief. Immediately, the handkerchief is tied to a rock, and buried without rites—not in an ocean, but in a calm fishbowl. Minus the fish, of course. They're coarse, that's why, swimming nude and breathing in an irregular way, through trap doors that open out of their shoulders with vulgar bravado. And no water in the bowl, either. And no bowl, either. Just the thought of a bowl. That should suffice.

He wouldn't even allow himself to be indifferent to women, but had to be less than indifferent. That almost verged on hostility, but he had none, so he didn't. He washes his hands of all things, and even throws his hands away, to avoid contaminating the silent recess of his soul. As for a blush, it's pure white. But he never blushes, anyway. He merely subdues the blood, filters it in the meaningless air, and internalizes the balance, thus leaving him void. Consulting his void, he secretly deals himself privacy, chaperoned by a spy, and consults the notions of silence. Who's to say if he's happy? Who's to say if he *is*? Indulging invisibility, he disappears frequently, and remains very slow about finding himself. He procrastinates, and watches days dwindling into hours, and microscopically vanishing beyond the pearly seconds. If any thought lingers, he's careful to keep it mystic. Not that he's a prude. He doesn't have enough guts to be one. All told, existence remains an impossibility, which he carefully cultivates. But doesn't encourage. No, he's too negative for that. He's so negative, he won't even say no. It's a concession if he even hints maybe. He allows himself no liberty. That would be rash of him, should he suddenly become free. Ungrateful, too.

So instead, he goes on thinking. And thinking. Not about, or even concerning. Subject matter is a waste, and drains his resources. He minimizes energy, and is the end product. The wasted force of a total world goes toward his stubborn denial. Then he slackens, and even denial is effete, having lost its juice of a positive being. The insubstantial is the new toy my friend plays at, with neither interest nor zest. My friend has slid down the limbo to an existence minor by all vital means. Even his disappearance is not entirely invisible. His whole is disintegrated, and recognition is dispersed into the nebulous particles of anonymity. No essence is granted the solidity of its elements. Evaporation shall tear apart my friend's fluid surface. The depth to remain is the colorless void.

Returning to the sanity of nature, my friend greeted me with an ample hello. Not knowing how to reply, and not daring to innovate, I stripped all caution aside, and left the answer hanging by its rafters in some corner of the upper air, frightfully near a spider's nest. Then, I proceeded to ignore him, and by that very means his proclaimed existence insisted on emphasis, like a lady scorned, or a widow spurned. As for the fury, I let it run itself out, and magnify its distraction concentrated behind inattentiveness, where memory, stumbling over a lost key, locked itself into nowhere, allowing the present moment to emerge inviolate, like innocence born on behalf of a baby and confined to an early cradle; where, under the mattress, a secret lady awaits, disguised as a snake, and, winning a losing apple, plunges the inmate into a roaring game of give and take, while the voice of the rattle is heard, and twin dice go gambling up and down the thumping board, obscuring the sound of clouds serenading the moon and escorting an early sun out of a premature eclipse. "How do you do?" I wagged at my friend, while he, chasing his own tail, was barking up a future tree, which, but for the forest, he couldn't see, and all the dangling leaves.

"What should we be caught doing?" he decided to ask me. I was at a loss, which he converted to a gain. Otherwise, we go broke. So he climbed down from that false tree, ripping off some paper leaves, and causing an entire forest to cease to be, like the life of a fly swatted out in a summer kitchen in a bungalow far away, in a wandering moment of our distant childhood, leaving the taste of mystery behind, an uncertain smell, and a deep impression. Here he was, and the tide of life moved on.

The next step was to go nowhere, where we had never been. Agreeing to meet later, we separated. The separation was mutual, and left us far apart.

Finally there remained to go nowhere. I was bashful, but in a determined sort of way. It was just up my alley. I had the map all charted. The map was lost, and so was I. So I had to retrace all my steps, and in the meanwhile, was my friend somewhere too? Yes, but out of sight.

To apologize for going nowhere, I had to hurry. On route, I met my friend walking in a similar, if not identical, direction. "The coincidence is all mine," he said gallantly. "No, it's on me," I begged to offer. The compromise delayed us both, so we returned to the starting point, heedless of our fate.

Now we vowed to keep together. It was only natural. As there was no sense in walking without a purpose, we deliberately set a destination, with the help of one of those upside down maps that are so careful to avoid being dogmatic in any specific direction. Under the handicap, we were auspicious. Which threatened to incapacitate us further, so we vowed to keep the same route together, mutually if possible, or else separately. Choices aren't always available, so we grab the next best thing that comes along, like a shot in the dark, and thus destiny is so intriguing. Like the wife you missed, so you go and actually meet your real one, who becomes a final substitute, culminating a series of direct impossibilities and probable near misses. No wonder we come out second best. Or third best, if there were three. Since with arithmetic there's no arguing, and numbers are absolutely inevitable, quantitatively linked, as they so definitely are, to the holy source of mystery, X marking that abandoned spot, the philosopher's quest and holy grail that unbinds the Gordian knot and answers the Sphinx's riddle with probably some abstruse pun. But back to the known. We were ready to start out, struggling to maintain an equal equality and so eliminate the disturbing factor of inequality relative to each other, at least from the start of things, other things being equal, or oddly poised to an uneven advantage, mutual to both. Oh, for exact Science!

I walked together with my friend. Keeping in step, we were soon both wearing the same shoes. Nevertheless, I slightly lagged behind. "Hurry, slowpoke," he called to me cheerfully. The scarce sun was becoming rationed, so there was only one shadow between us. We shared it like brothers who marry the same girl and celebrate with two distinct honeymoons. Being more selfish than either of us, he took them both, while I stayed home to mind the kitchen.

At length, we stopped to rest. But he was at the destination, and I at the starting point. This showed how impossible it was to agree. We vowed to impose opposite turns on any future mutual direction. Even to diverge lifetimes, if possible, giving him an early century, and me bringing up the future rear.

* * *

My friend traveled. First he went one place, and then another. I met him everywhere. "Where are you?" we asked, and for answer we traveled somewhere else, mainly to avoid coming to a definite geographical conclusion. We went every which way, and each new place was exactly like a homecoming. The further we went, the closer we were to always returning, until returning became identified as just an extension of our very broad traveling, which took us so far that we were as close and near to being in the same place as though motion, though including everything else, had declined to take us on board, leaving us still, so still that even time paused to catch a hurried breath. "Where are we now?" I asked. "Look and see," said my friend, for he also didn't know. It was strange how everyplace always has one location, going or coming, and that location is at the paralyzed center from which we never move, despite all external evidence to the contrary. "I'm tired, let's stop," I announced. "So soon?" said my friend, while accumulating his momentum. As he flew off, I flew off, determining to counteract his futile act of going. On the way, we met, and as our passed croth, we looked neither behind nor ahead, but were busily involved, tensing the wing to its furthermost stretch, in being there where now we are, and used such a slow speed that time declined to compete. "Hurry," I said, mainly to myself. After arriving, we found we weren't there, and so had to go all the way back, a tedious journey, just to take ourselves with us, a useless and unnecessary baggage that would only slow up the whole works. Being human, how could we get anywhere? "I'm right behind you," said my friend, a very deceiving statement.

* * *

My friend underwent a mild confusion between where time went and where he went. Not to mention the means, or "how." To resolve these eternal complications, and solve their strange flowings, he recapitulates by declaring these plain statements, cut down to such language as arrests motion into the formalized convention of simplicity's deceptive nonsense:

"I went away, and came back too late. This upset my whole schedule.

"At the last minute, I transferred to a bus. By then, the airplane was still in flight.

"The train will arrive.

"I consult time, but as it is always in motion, I hesitate to draw a conclusion.

"Time vanished, and in my pursuit, I became a traveler.

"But I went the wrong way. Now I have to wait for it to catch up.

"I attached time to my wrist, and hold the arm still, to check the course of blood. Outside, though, it still rages.

"I'm related to time through my grandfather clock. If he dies, others will take his place.

"Of course, there's not only time. There's me."

* * *

A clock was wasting time, going around in empty circles, and pointing a pair of idle hands into a whole rotation of directions, without really getting anywhere. The movement was deathlike in its deliberation, and kept repeating itself until, in a short while, it was never done. Like a lover so solitary he never dates anyone else, it's going steady, and doesn't the least know when to stop, which is immoral. My friend is that clock, which is so alarming he's threatened to be awakened any minute now, provided it's not too late. "Oh, it's *never* too late," he says, answering from his uninterrupted sleep, as if from memory, since his brain is counterclockwise and has fallen far, far behind, almost to the original point of antiquity, when the past was just freshly preparing to begin.

* * *

All at once, everything happened. "Not so fast," my friend yelled, trying to keep up with the action, since it was already too late to participate. Then time, prompt as usual, put an end to these events, and left my bewildered friend in an acute state of retrospect, which was his only weapon against the past but had no practical application for his current life. "What went on?" I asked just as soon as I arrived. My friend stared at me, unable even to approach a reply. "Oh," I said.

* * *

"Today is the most modern day in the whole world," informed my friend. I looked up a historical atlas, observed dates of the liveliest events, nostalgically pined for the golden cave age, and looked at the slowed-up dial in the carcass of a clock whose soul had been smitten by a heart attack. "You mean just now?" I asked, striving to ascertain the most exact correctitude. The sun paused in the process of distilling a ray.

Agreeing that today was not only modern, but even *avant-garde* (French, which is to say, That it is ahead of our time), I bothered to inhale a double-barreled dose of the latest air, fresh from the atmosphere. I breathed it out stale, but that's a story for another day.

As we were witnessing the scene, like preview gate crashers at the newest repeat performance of a fashion show currently in vogue, the moon replaced the sun. This blackened up the sky considerably, and reversed our opinion about "modern." "We have regressed," informed my friend, and bawled like a prenatal precocious baby. "That's funny, I feel senile," I announced, and grew a wooden cane from the obsolete middle leg that had dried up. In our contrary methods, we found an identical kingdom, that of the time-nullifier, sleep. Awaking, we saw a very secondhand day paused on the top of a cloud. The lack of originality appalled us.

* * *

My friend developed an inordinate appetite for excess, pushing this unyielding passion to sublimely ridiculous extravagance, even to such lengths as to go immoderately beyond the rim of overboard, whole-hog, demonic, obsessive. Later, it cost him.

Chastised, he hung his head down, and now takes a puny step forward, and a puny step backward, to blot himself out. To be extra moderate, he stands still in between, safe behind four equal walls of humdrum balance. This life teaches him in slow degrees the art of becoming a stone. Now he barely vegetates on the border of a mineral, he who used to be so animate. He regresses through evolution, sliding back further than the history of the sun, in his almost pathetic obedience to the spirit of a death wish. "At the rate you're going," I warned him, "you're ruining your whole existence." In answer, his bones jutted forth another inch to the surface of his skin. The flesh was growing inward, to be devoured where his core sloped in pith to an endless pit. A few young ashes were seen emerging like spring plants from his convenient outlets that once proudly launched forth his evermost pleasures. Pity dragged from me a maternal sob, which his sense nerve was now luxuriously equipped to ignore. "Is there a moral to this?" I prayed, and browsed through an overhead bible hanging in an open sky, whose rotating pages unfurled their braille mystery from the sightless ceiling, which our agony compels us to pretend to read.

* * *

Although he was now feeling quiet, and had a silent sensation, my friend was still very much talking, producing a rapid sequence of automatic words that were swiftly spent past his own awareness, hurrying on out of his responsibility. I began answering him, and even mildly argued on some of his more questionable remarks, challenging his opinions, and returning the conversation on its points of articulate balance. "What's going on?" he demanded, implying insanity on my part. His eyes became circles, arched by wide quizzical brows underlined with a strength of tact. "As you were saying—," I answered. "Said what? Who?" he calmly asked, ready, if necessary, to give me the humorous benefit of a smile. Then a hostile silence issued from his lips, which had the merit of being obvious, and he won the point. What could I say to that soundless triumph, that was now cleverly erasing the words he claimed he never spoke? My ears are on the modest side, willing to doubt an echo while pushing it into the tide of memory. Time has always been my weakness. I believe the present, but am quite an atheist when it comes to trusting the past. To remain real, a former thing has got to be repeated, otherwise it draws a blank and is suavely passed over by my mind. "Let me tell you something," my friend began, and though my ears were slow to cooperate, I quickly assembled my attention. I listened with all my power, and tasted the impact of every separate syllable. "How flattering," my friend thought, inwardly, while the sentences curled from his face like smoke about to vanish in the blue. Their cargo of ideas dented my understanding, and proceeded to withdraw their proof. When the assault was over, my friend paused. The air grew thick and solid between us, pregnant with some great impending abortion. "You agree, don't you," he said, his arms of communication about to enclose their embrace on me. Then a hush, as my answer was prepared. He was waiting. The eyes quickened, the breath sped through the interval, clashing with the unknown. At last I stirred my tongue, the lips began to open, teeth had to be recognized. "Hello," I said; "Where have you been all this while? And tell me, how goes it? Come on. What's on your mind, these days?" "I'm fine, thank you," he said, "and have been meaning to talk to you. Great things are happening. Listen. I want your opinion." "Were you away?" I interrupted. "Completely," he said; "You have no idea." "Go on, then," I begged, "I'm dying to hear." "Not so fast," he said. "Why?" "You're too damn curious, that's why." Stubborn, we both stopped. On this, we were fully in accord. By mutual consent, the whole record, spoken and unspoken, was forgotten so deeply, nothing remains from the nothing that ever transpired. My friend stopped existing, and my own existence went into decline where it spends most of its time, suspended among sounds neither heard nor made, and assured by uncertainty.

* * *

I said to my friend, "The moon shines," and he, not to be outdone, reminded me that the sun is so hot that it burns the hours away. "So that's what happened to them!" I replied, since I remembered many hours which were not with me anymore. And so we both held up the same smile, as though it were a valise containing stubs of matinee and evening performances in the theatre of life.

Later on, holding another conversation with the same friend, I told him what a simple pleasure it was to marvel at the absent sea. I expected him to ask, "What absent sea?" Since he didn't, and with a dry throat, I asked permission to fetch a bottle. He generously took out two glasses, and after refilling, we reflected that the bottle was empty. "Is that the absent sea?" he asked. "Yes," I answered, while a whale lunged about in my stomach.

Our next conversation, like a stained glass window, reflected guilty religion. We gossiped about angels, like boys who talk about movie actors. "Ever seen an angel?" he asked, his voice purring with simple faith. "Not since I *was* one," I answered, which stunned us into incredible silence. Once the silence was removed, like an unruly drunk from a dignified tavern, we traded words, like an Oriental Indian trading ivory tusks to an American Indian in exchange for a twenty-four-dollar elevator ride across the Brooklyn Bridge. Feeling better, we relieved ourselves by eating. Then, while he went to the bathroom, I sat back and succeeded deliciously in not thinking. He returned, though, to interrupt my non-train of thought. Angry, I called him a name that reflected poorly on his mother. He agreed with me. As we were shaking hands, though, winter turned into spring, and spring bloomed into very summer. We decided to close the window. But nature never slowed down. It ran around in dizzy circles, chasing the leaves up and down the tree. The clock, feeling pulse and rhythm, stirred in its wicked blood. The panic beat in my breast like a storm.

Our last conversation in this series, of course, summed up everything. In the broadest general terms, we spread philosophy like a carpet (or rug) across the living room floor of the world (or life). Anything in our way, we swept under the rug using a bold broom with sweeping authority. At last we both concluded that we knew even less than Plato. This flattered our concept of ignorance, but made our knowledge feel inferior. For compromise, we turned on a television set. It was a book program. The words were big. We would read them across the screen, and when we reached the bottom of the page, the announcer's hand turned to the next one. It fascinated us. Little by little, our ignorance was getting drunk. After the end of the book, the announcer explained the plot. He was a nice man. His voice was gentle for its size. It was lovely. We soon fell asleep. What my friend dreamed, I don't know. My dream was about his dream. Lacking information, and frankly respecting his privacy, I had to make my dream blank, just like the void before the world began. In another hour I expect to wake up. I am comfortable. I love to have no pain. The sun burns up another hour. I feel myself exploding. I wake up like a drunk fish, and roar into the bathroom. Then I go back, and my friend is not dead. Realizing this, I watch him wake up. Covering me with his eye, he yawns a hole so wide that horses and men and all other creatures rush through. When the storm subsides, a peaceful serenity sails through the room. "Are you awake?" I ask. "No," he replies, waiting for my smile to reach its peak. Let him wait.

* * *

"Say," said my friend, "won't you talk philosophy with me? It's such an interesting topic, when one gets down to it. One can discuss it for hours, and still never get anywhere. Shall we?" I said yes, and we went all over philosophy, backwards to front and top to side again, without knowing quite what was being talked about. "That was wonderful," said my friend, after we had enough; "like to do it again next time?" "Sure, it's fun," I agreed, and felt a nice kind of laziness, sort of soft and easy, as though my brain were soaking in a hot tub. "Boy, what my mind went through," I said for my own ears, "lucky I still have it left. Hope its powers aren't impaired." So I decided to test it. I gave it arithmetic, which it added right. Next I had it spell a hard word, and it was almost perfect, missing just two letters. It was time to try humor. "Say something at me," I told my friend, "that I can reply to." So he said something, and I gave such a witty retort, he would have positively burst for laughing if he had only listened, but his attention was extracted.

"Don't mind me now, but I was only being funny," I said to him sarcastically, with just a dash of spite to recall his thoughts from their woolen trade. "Oh, were you?" I could see him say, with his mouth hanging open and a flabby bit of his tongue sort of sticking out in the center, awed by all the stupidity it had to unload and all the verbal traffic it had to handle as a shipping clerk with the minimum time out for a coffee break. He looked dumb, and it frightened me. "Philosophy you want?" he asked, and before I could wake up the whole room was dense and packed with philosophy, so we could hardly move. I managed to open a window, to give the philosophy a little air and ourselves an excuse to breathe. But a stiff wind blew, upsetting my friend's theories and spilling the wisdom in slippery splashes all about the room, where puddles of nonsense formed and the sloppy mud of logic.

"You spoiled everything," my friend accused me. "Well, I was only trying to be constructive," I apologized, while guilt tugged at my emotions from the opposite end. "You toy with philosophy," my friend said, in an angry mood: "Thoughts are serious, and some thoughts are immortal. Wise men wasted all their lives making them up. And now you come along, like an innocent wise guy, and blow it all to pieces, with your cheap vanity and your clever dynamite and your brainless lazy hatred for beauty and truth. The world will get even on you. Man hasn't come this far for you to make a monkey of him. All you think of is sex, like a neurotic amoeba in the first place. God won't let you get away with this. If you think *Christ* was punished, wait till you see what happens to *you*. Three to one you land in hell, and make a continual ash of yourself. I'll help you go there, because I like to see justice on top." Apparently he was angry. Till his mood would change, I'd help him to silent treatment. Silence enraged him further. He attacked it with every word he had, like an army invading an enemy with a complete arsenal of any legal or unlegal warfare instrument, and any word that didn't exist he made up as he went along, invoking the President's wartime emergency powers of totalitarian tyranny and arch dictatorship to concentrate on the total necessity of winning the peace. Only exhaustion could stop him, which it did. "I'm insulted!" I said. Then we signed an unconditional armistice, which gave us time to bury me with martial rites. "How dead I am," I said, at the last minute. "Take it philosophically,' he advised, and became one with the hammer that drove me through the nail to make the coffin perfect for its headlong dive. Down I went, through dead layers of philosophy—outworn metaphysics, logical ashes, alcohol-preserved theology, ugly aesthetic remnants, ethical bones, dusty destiny, the dungeon of free will, Utopian failure, and that ultimate theoretical, speculative, absurdity-reduced Nothingness, touchstone of the ages. Thus I was one with the earth-treasured hoard of man's darkest wisdom, accumulated from the opening moment of time. This made me undoubtedly wise, if only I could have known, or troubled to pass a thought through this transcendental magic. But I hadn't one atom left in me, and was, for all eternity, a material waste.

* * *

My friend has a lifelong guarantee. It beings when he was born, and ends whenever "Now" is. This leaves his future up to chance, but his risky life delights him. Feeling like a pirate about to escape from walking the plank, or like a last-minute-saved would-be victim of an execution squad whose smoking guns turn from fact to mirage, my friend pinches his mirror, where he is convinced his flesh actually grows.

One day, a cemetery salesman knocked on his door, and wanted to sell him a plot. My friend almost reversed the table, by trying to kill the man-about-business, whose half-choked neck flirted briefly with immortality or damnation on behalf, primarily, of the rest of him. Next day, the cemetery had a fire sale, then closed down for want of recruits. The ghosts were transferred to "senior citizen" homes, a social come-down for most. They talked in lively tones about old age, the consensus of opinion being that old age was a hazard. The discussion waxed merrily. For reinforcement, marshmallows were served. But not before some practical joker had toasted them almost to a crisp. Elsewhere in the world, life plunged out of a billion wombs.

Inside my friend, where it hurts, is lodged his skeleton. His most durable feature, it lives for the day when it may make its naked debut. My friend wishes to cover up this scandal, but for all his fancy clothing and well-haired skin, his defense is slipping. A psychoanalyst, whose specialty is depth, concluded that my friend is "repressing" his skeleton. But if this personal trauma should ever emerge, my friend could barely survive it.

* * *

One morning I greeted my friend. "Hi," I said, warm and cheerful, like the sun. "Hi," he replied, and smiled with gentle generosity, having suddenly discovered that he could afford it, following a self-depriving lifetime of tight stinginess with its miserly withholding of simple free humanity and the dear virtues that cost nothing. "Where were you?" I asked. "Oh, I was plotting something in the cemetery for a rainy day, and I met an old fellow—real conservative, if not a reactionary in the flesh—who said he liked first things first, preferring the order of precedence, and so he always took one step and followed with the other rather than reversing the primary etymology of such a procedure, and for the same reason liked mothers better than children and causes better, consequently, than their frequently mistaken consequences determined scientifically as 'effects.' His tastes reverted back also. He couldn't stand any painting since the golden era of Cimabue or music since the divine Palestrina or literature after lord Homer or civilization since the origin of miraculous Utopia, or gods since the basic establishment of the atom-like amoeba (that indivisible nutshell that sometimes, in splitting, goes to hell), preceding the enterprising colonization of advanced evolution as we know it today, in its self-deteriorating forms of explosive modern violence which Darwin, not having known how the worst was to come, repents of and mourns continually, anticipating a terrible showdown. And this fellow I met, he knew ancient languages as well, and was so adept at the caveman's grunt in particular that you wouldn't know him from a native in both the archaic and recent dialects, conserving the authentically original syntax and enlivening the inflection-void obsoleteness of all that incarnately dead as well as extinct vocabulary, the nucleus of 'thought' as we know it today. He was gifted, with such a background. He picnicked in graveyards and took photos of ghosts in old-fashioned poses leaning against their ineradicable epitaphs with the sun shining clean through them and getting their pictures taken in the transparent liveliness of their ever youthful eternities, smiling for the fled bird that early flew to catch the surprise morning worm in the round glow of a constant horizon ringing our fate, spreading out a never-fading dawn to beautify the otherwise lugubrious aspects of the photo-picnic. Nevertheless, afternoon arrived, and when the milk soured, the cheese went moldy, the pears grew senile, and the grapes dried out into black raisins, the ghosts rioted and refused to return to the norm and sanity of home sweet grave till their guest developed his photos to show them their forbidden images of outraged desolate humanity, the scourges of their ravished past, which soon discouraged all thought of rebellion, and led them to subside into peaceful rank, swear off the haunting life, and vanish into an unseen dimension, leaving not a trace nor an autograph behind to substantiate the old fellow's overworldly excursion into the remote underground, the precinct of his pre-exploration in the interests of the unwritable history to come, man's self-archaeology, ruins ruminating over ruins, decadence discovering decay, brainless skulls peering into the vacuum of bones and souls hidden in tears by the shameless earth, gaily weeping and fertilizing the tragedy to yield an astounding crop of the buried dead and the unburied living, twins disunited briefly between murders inflicted by time on all the citizens of space, granting us a respite in the shaded sanctuary of Today, where, with the focus on us, we yet pant and bide a little while, secure in the passage of this permanent brevity, the still landscape focused in the canvas of that minute, and the next hour, and perhaps tomorrow." "Was the fellow very old?" I asked my friend. "How relative do you mean?" was his quick reply. "I don't get you," I said. "That is, everything seems old, don't you think?" my friend explained. "You yourself?" I asked. "Now you're getting personal," he said, and shook what sadly remained of all the tattered glory of his head. "I'll proceed to illustrate," he said, and wandered over that age-old theme, delineating the forms of dying, the extremes of growing old:

"Growing old is quite an experience. But it can be overdone.

"A man overdid it for years. When we last heard from him, he was an archaeologist in search of himself.

"The moon is an old-timer, too. When last seen, it was heard muttering, "Them durn waves!"

"But speaking of age, how about water? I know a raindrop that started to come down from a cloud. But by the time it arrived, the poor old thing was so dry it didn't even tickle.

"The earth is bulging with dead people. Cemeteries are so costly, they're building them in skyscrapers today. On the top floor, you have a penthouse view of God.

"And do you think God is so young? It's a marvel He survives!

"But He does, of course. The old Fool comes out every Sunday.

Crumbled up in a weak rocking chair, He stares with vacant eyes against the virile sun. Patches of His shadow, meanwhile—the clergy—preach for Him.

"People are born so quick they die even faster. Like actors in a hurry, they run onto the stage and run off. And they not only forget their lines but there's no time to even remember them. Hamlets change into Yoricks, and the soliloquy you hear is really a chorus. And the audience is on stage too, laughing tombwise, while the merry tears go frolicking down just as the face vanishes and a skull emerges. Holy terror, what a fate!

"Not for me, of course. I plan to watch the mirror. And die of eyestrain just as the hair turns grey."

"Do me a favor," I said, "and reveal your age: it's haunting me." To evade the question, he almost died right then. I pursued him to the ultimate verge, and yelled for him to return. "Why? Maybe it's better I go on," he said. "No, don't do that, it's bad for you," I warned, and, taken aback, my friend called up his ultimatum, suggesting I give a reason, using my art of the manly philosophy of persuasion to dangerously recall him from the leaping peak of his dire precipice. "Wait, wait," I said, and launched into:

"Death is the dreariest discord. It occurs at the end of life. It creates a radical change, but works for the negative.

"Nobody wants it. At best, it is an unnecessary evil. At worst—but it has no worst."

"That convinces me," my friend said, returning to the world alive. "I'm back to avoid my death. If the worst wants me, let it seek me out later; I refuse to volunteer, since death would cancel my egotism and rob me of my image. While I've a reputation to go by, I'll still stay as I am. If death *lusts* after me, let her wear a seductive robe woven of time's trailing thread. Just yet, it's too early for her plunder of my virtue."

* * *

My friend's infantile fear is to die when asleep. Hence his morbid precautions:

"I only sleep superficially, because beyond a certain point sleep mixes with death—and that's dangerous. With one eye, I keep watch. If my sleep goes down too deep through its plunge of nightmares, out comes a waking dream to snatch me into the jaws of safety. Like a survivor panting on shore, I inhale a sunbeam, drink the honeyed dew of pearly morn, and let the early day devour my soft gratitude. The sunken ship behind me rises, and floats to the dock, waiting for night to drug me aboard. So I must sail, a regular subject to a drowsy risk that threatens my hold on nature."

* * *

My friend and I were about to die, but we didn't know who would go first. "Go ahead," I said, politely making room. But he was too feeble to move, and I, with my senile wanderings, was too futile to insist. It was a stalemate, and meanwhile life was getting scarce, and barely enough breath still existed to fulfill our competitive greed. "Both at once?" I suggested, touched by this dramatic final proof of our devotion, friendship's fatal loyalty even to its termination and perhaps beyond. "Let's stay," my friend answered, his grin toothless and his teeth grinless. Then he coughed. I sighed, and continually lost weight. Space began to get fat, at our own very expense. Time was getting fat, feeding on our lifelong remnants to the very last burp. It was all over, we should give up. "Now?" I asked again. "Pardon, I'm deaf now," my friend replied, and he was right. Oh, he was so right. Meanwhile, light stopped, which meant blindness. "Are you prepared?" I asked. His perfect answer was to not hear, which I deemed very fitting. "You're invisible," I said. Again, he resumed his right to not hear. And pretty soon, I should be right.

I was going, he was going. There was no stopping us, our minds were made up. Off we went, and then we forgot.

By the time we were gone, a last regret tried to reclaim us. "You're too late," I contrived to let out, while speech had passed from faltering to impaired. Obedient, the regret subsided, and just at that very moment, I had no friend, and my friend had me no longer. Like substance itself, as though endowed with a purpose, and concerned with the destinies of its joint owners, the friendship withdrew its heart from functionary blood-pumping, and left a bundle of crumbling bones to give its memory a formal representation in the world, scene of its self-proclaimed triumph, comic drama, infernal conflict, resumptions, surprises, string of consolations, fierce ingratitudes, patchquilt reparations, storms of humanity, deceitful truths and mood-compelled delusions, tear-stifling laughter, harsh panics of joy, crushed sensibility, enormous agony, peephole revelations, spiritual vagaries and indefinitions, divine nonsense, and that pathetic irony of it all, gospelfirm sincerity. The friendship emerged, then, as its own tragedy, independent of mine, independent of my friend's, having survived neither of us, the sunken center of that trio.

* * *

After I died, I tried to resume friendship with my friend, which would console me and take the sting off my self-bereavement, and perhaps, in some distant way, afford me compensation. I looked around, but could only see the lack of myself, which stood out, almost visibly, against a background conspicuous for its emptiness. "Are you there?" I hollered, not at all loudly. I got the answer I deserved, a windblown nothingness that roared through the ears I didn't have. This increased my loneliness, and I went in search for tears, hoping to fit them against some stray eyes that I should light upon, to fabricate the semblance of weeping, which might magically create emotion. Then only me would be necessary for me to completely live again, in the usual fashion, and nostalgia would revert painfully to its realistic origin, converting this useless death to the former misery and mere wish for death by which my body's small hours were dominated mentally.

* * *

My friend was certainly not immune to death, so he died. Happening to be dead myself at the time, I was in a deeply sympathetic position, ideally, and my vantage point afforded, potentially, the maximum understanding. The drawback was that I couldn't utilize this advantage. Thus our friendship entered a perpetual equality, which gave every indication of remaining so for the length of its infinite duration. Justice was distrib-

uted with handsome, liberal abundance, by which we were mutually over-
come, done in, depleted, castrated, undone, crucified, revenged, opened
up, augmented, injured, completed, washed up, thrown away, stepped
on, fouled, besmirched, violated, outraged, killed outright, murdered
irrevocably, shot at, hung, pinched, choked, smothered, raped, crapped
upon, done away with, shanghaied, kidnapped, unransomed, curtailed,
truncated, imposed upon, de-energized, shriveled up, diminished, and
rendered invisible. We were at an end, done for, and that horrid actuality passed, and has become continually true ever since, increasing as
time goes by, with its regular weekly Wednesdays and other outstanding
events. As deprived ex-citizens, we no longer participate in these super-
ficial calendar festivities and decadent accumulation of annual year-by-
years, but rather are immersed, or blended rather, in our full loss.

* * *

When my friend died, he traditionally applied for heaven. "Sold out," he
was told. Caught in an embarrassing position without his body, which
had been a favorite possession of his, despite its average selection of pain
and its minority indulgence of pleasure, he became a drifter, a tramp in
space, a floater idle to the virtues of time, as he was indifferent to the
fluctuating power and richly uncertain values of money. Down on his
luck, he was arrested for loitering, or being parked on an illegal cloud on
an alternate rainy day. The court scene was blinding as abstract justice
was administered in an offhand manner that barely reflected the crime,
assuming there was one. My friend had to move over, and get going.
The stars set off a beautiful night, the planets described their ornamental orbits, meteors and portent signs showed off their flashy Broadway
jewelry that deceives the tourist with meaningless symbols like modern literary criticism. My friend felt like a candle wandering through
a Christmas tree whose glittering electric pagan angels trapped the literal imagination into hysterical pogroms of commercial festivity, sheer
holiday mass tastelessness in a setting of colored tin and wired sound.
"I shouldn't have died," my friend regretted, displaying his usual tardy
wisdom that ripens to self-assertion just when practical application is
impossible. "My luck is bad all over, I guess," he said, shrugging the

shoulders he no longer had and lifting those former eyebrows, that came in handy when expression needed something extra. "The good old days," he pined, while cosmic nostalgia assaulted his soul.

* * *

What happened to time, after my friend died? It simply sidestepped him, and went in another direction; and now my friend is trying to live again, and is seeking to identify himself with time's personality, but time, like a former lover who's forgotten the whole business, maintains its new impersonal distance, as if there was never any involvement in the first place, and if there had been, so what of it? This was disastrous for my friend, he mourned with a broken heart, and all his jilted flesh and bones put up a dismal cry of protest, while the stars never flinched, and time gave her favors to other—but new—lovers. "They were lucky to be born late," my friend said of them, as though to have been early was to have been never. "How hard it is," he went on, "after such a quick and unsatisfactory life, like an act of sex with an aborted orgasm, to have to be outside of it all, way outside, with not even a soul to console me spiritually, and never participate, and be always scorned by time." Thus he said, but not existing, he could impart no substance to the words, being forever lost to sound, and unrelated to any sense. Such vivid emotions he once had, such blind intensity had been his life, the failure of love and hate, the defeat of intellect. He was a vehicle for pain, a recipient of unexpected pleasure, and the victim of his own gradual retirement from everything he had been. If only time could be replaced, or if deeply hoped-for magic could reward his despair with one small timely personal little birth! How he would recover! How he would be grateful!

* * *

"Good lord, how I hate to be dead," my friend's angel announced. "Yes, it's bitter," I agreed. "Do you remember that girl I used to date?" he said. "Oh yes," I replied, pretending that I did. "Well, I wonder what she's doing now," came that sad tone. "Married, probably," I vagued to estimate. "Children?" "Suppose." The silence deepened.

"We had a great deal of fun," my friend ventured forth again. "Most likely you did," and I couldn't hide my boredom. Nothing is so deadly, I thought, as a couple of fellows without their bodies fooling around with the remnants of sensual memory. First of all, it wasn't appropriate. Then, nothing practical, in this world or the former, could be gained by it. A shallow waste, wasting the breath of eternity. "Forget about her," I advised, though it seemed heartless; "try to be independent, for once. Useless to mourn over spilt life. What are you, a tragedian? Why don't you get down to earth?—I mean down to this place," and I blushed, while the echo of my mistake rang through the dismal vacancy. How harsh. Reality is nowhere appreciated, neither there nor here. Ideals follow us through both worlds, like camp-followers to a marching army, the painted tramps, homeless, that beg to be taken in, warmed over, and destroyed with caress. Death has no benefits. It's very disillusioning.

"She had pretty lips," my friend said, "and heartless eyes, and breathtaking breasts, and well-divided legs, and soft golden feelings everywhere, a headful of vanity, and a capacity to absorb my love until unheard-of reserves would be called forth, love so actual you could touch it, and then forgo the use of those fingers that had done the touching; the fingers would be mounted up on the wall and embalmed, enshrined as commemorative trophies of those minute-hour-week-month-years that experience converted into things too real to be snapped up by this sanitary oblivion that bathes and bathes our souls clean through, till we're just transparencies for the sun's endless image by which nature undergoes its usual renewal as a service to tardy children who have the good fortune to be ever continually born late." "Why couldn't that happen to us?" I said, and the pang of being cheated by an early birth became a fresh sensation, if these formless thoughts we think in this vaporless atmosphere can ever be confused with living sensations. "Ah, life," I moaned: "there's really no substitute for it."

For a minute we were quiet. "I can make love all over again," boasted my bodiless friend, "if only I put on a little weight." "Problems!" I sneered: "don't come to me with your problems." But secretly I was wishing the same thing myself. Amazing how similar we've become. That's the trouble with death: no individuality.

Once he was dead, my friend regretted it. "I must make a comeback," he determined, like an athletic figure temporarily ensnared by middle age and, in a weak moment, given over to fatty layers of soft tissue as a kind of negligent favor to a down-and-out friend whom he had always denied. Death was unusual, after so much life. It made him blink, though the eye with its umbrella of hair had packed up the sight and long vanished. Cool, he felt, like a nervous system left in the freezer overnight but detached from a body that could have complained. Idle, he was, like a businessman on a strictly imposed pension diet, yearning for that visionary isle, his office. Not existing had its limitations, but my friend just had to make the most of them, in a sparse spirit of spare denial. Those were lean times. Bound to do without, my friend learned the grammar of minimums, a language which he thoroughly perfected (despite its lack of vocabulary), observing especially the refined syntax of multiple negatives. Although by no means happy, my friend wasn't unhappy, either. Thus he canceled himself out, and enjoyed freedom from irksome extremes. How easy moderation was now. By force of memory, my friend smiled, though lacking the facial equipment. No rebellion, no protest. And so his death, with his consent, reached a firmer finality. "Someone must have hammered another nail on the underground coffin," he thought, as though he could see outside himself, like a blind man developing mystic inclinations to make up for the poverty of his sensations, and thereby claiming equality with men of great fame, such as God. "What a habit this is," he said, speaking of his own death with a kind of detachment he had always in vain striven for during those confused days of his life. Adjusted to the regularity of his death, he achieved his old talent for the mediocre, and was absorbed into a vast commonplace. But unusual for him, the harmony was complete.

* * *

My friend was a man of culture. He belonged to Western Civilization of the post-caveman era, at the point of intersection between Christianity and Chaos, when the world was organizing its billion unities into one central vacuum, an astronomical self-deity fully regulated for the convenience of the individual man, including the latest catastrophes of science and the flush overgrown flowering of art's decadence. Although belonging to this crucial turning point in the history of evolution, marking a vast advancement beyond the state of primitive flowers, my friend was too self-conscious to appreciate or fear this. Absorbed in his own universal life, he was unaware of the provincial cosmos, with its monotonously regular sun that appeared quite content to shine forever. Surrounded by such negative things as death, my friend was restored to the total glory of his depth by that dark subjective mirror, psychology, through which his commonplace mind became timelessly identified with cultural landmarks like God, that raised his subsistence to an unprecedented standard of what was then called living. This was true for his whole tribe, the barbaric remnants of an outmoded spiritual materialism. None of nature survived. He was a man of his time, my good friend and true. Seen against the outline of history, those customs, stale rites, and broad traditions, those institutions with their built-in guarantees of permanence, take on a distinct quaint flavor, and seem infinitely worthy of our study. At last, those bead-like days have arranged themselves into just that perspective required for our thorough manipulation of the past. We snatch them out of time, and arrest their flowing moment. That antique animal, my friend.

* * *

"Was my life real?" my friend's soul said in muted retrospect. "Sure it was! For what am I doing dead now, otherwise? Death is only strong and permanent when it feeds on real life. And so, at last I know," and the smile sailed confidently up the heavens and through time's revolving door, and then Inside, where history could pursue him no longer and his story's last page gave its reluctant end on the final Word.

ACKNOWLEDGMENTS

The publisher would like to thank the following individuals for their generous financial support which helped to defray some of this book's production costs: Becky, Brian R. Boisvert, D. Capobianco, Dave and Joan Carr, Shane Jesse Christmass, Martin Georgi, Leo F. Gray, Beverly Jean Harris, Maureen Crowley Heil, Morgan Hobbs, Peter and Deborah Jackson, Haya K., Eleonora Leto, Buck and Nadine Lombard, J.D. Lowry, Corinne Lyman, Sidney McMahon, Judy Mintz, Mark S. Mitchell, Thurston Moore, Colin Myers, Bob Plourde, Poems-For-All, Matthew J. Rogers, Frank V. Saltarelli, AJ Snyder, Svein, and Pamela Twining

ABOUT THE AUTHOR

Marvin Cohen is an American essayist, novelist, playwright, poet, humorist, and surrealist. He is the author of nine published books and several plays. His short fiction and essays have appeared in more than 80 publications, including *The New York Times, The Village Voice, The Nation, Harper's Bazaar, Vogue, Fiction, The Hudson Review, Quarterly Review of Literature, Transatlantic Review,* and New Directions annuals. His 1980 play *The Don Juan and the Non-Don Juan* was first performed at the New York Shakespeare Festival as part of the Poets at the Public Series. Staged readings of the play have featured actors Richard Dreyfuss, Keith Carradine, Wallace Shawn, Jill Eikenberry, Larry Pine, and Mimi Kennedy.

Born in Brooklyn in 1931, Cohen has described himself as one who has "risen from lower-class background to lower-class foreground." He studied art at Cooper Union but left college to focus on writing, supporting himself with a series of odd jobs including mink farmer and merchant seaman. He also taught creative writing at The New School, the City College of New York, C.W. Post of Long Island University, and Adelphi University. Cohen currently lives in New York City with his wife, a retired paperback editor.

www.ingramcontent.com/pod-product-compliance
Lightning Source LLC
Chambersburg PA
CBHW072117230425
25588CB00044B/276